Blues for the Buffalo

MANUEL RAMOS

Blues for the Buffalo

◆

St. Martin's Press
New York

Mystery
RAM

Library of Congress Cataloging-in-Publication Data

Ramos, Manuel.
    Blues for the buffalo / Manuel Ramos.
        p.   cm.
    ISBN 0-312-15480-1
    I. Title.
    PS3568.A4468B57   1997
    813' .54—dc21   96-52572
                                              CIP

First Edition: May 1997

10 9 8 7 6 5 4 3 2 1

FOR ZETA

C/S

1

$\blacklozenge$

W hat an ugly scar."

I opened my eyes into the brilliant Mexican sun. The details of her face were masked in a numbing combination of light and more light created by the sun and the white beach that curved against the turquoise lagoon.

"It must have hurt."

I shielded my eyes with the flat of my hand. Her skin recalled the *café con leche* I had nursed at breakfast. She wore a white two-piece swimsuit that was less than a bikini and she looked hot and sweaty.

"It hurt like hell. I was in the hospital for weeks. I still limp."

I raised a beer to my lips. My empty hand slipped from the handle of the cooler and grazed the hot sand and recoiled automatically. Her feet were naked, exposed to the sand.

"Is the bullet still in your knee?"

I did not ask how she knew it was a bullet wound. Maybe it was obvious.

"A fragment. But let's not talk about my knee. My name's Luis Montez."

I extended my hand and she intertwined her fingers among mine.

"Rachel Espinoza. I'm Philip's neighbor, when I can work it out. I saw you yesterday after the cab let you off. My place is up the road. Philip lets me use his beach."

Small world.

My unresponsiveness did not deter her, although I could hear a reluctance in her words. Maybe she thought she had to be polite by carrying on a conversation. She continued in a voice that brought a sadness to the edge of the ocean.

"You must be his lawyer friend from Denver. He told me you were coming. Told me how you two met. When he was still a cop. He tried to arrest your girlfriend for murder. He likes to talk about that case. I think he fell for her, even though she shot somebody."

"I'm not sure about that."

"That he got turned on by her, or that she shot somebody?"

"I don't think it was murder. That was a long time ago. A real long time ago."

"I guess you don't want to talk about it?"

"Whatever. I'm trying to get some rest. I've had a bad year. I don't mind the company, but I probably won't say much. You know how it is."

"Oh, yeah. I know."

A sigh of relief slipped into the tropical air and I was not sure if it had come from her or me.

She stretched belly down on a white blanket, turned her neck, and looked up at me. The two-piece had disappeared into the blanket. The sun and heat played tricks with my eyes and I had a difficult time concentrating. She shimmered, disjointedly. Her bronzed legs, shoulders, and arms leaped from the whiteness in a three-dimensional jiggle of distorted flesh.

I remembered a time when I would have asked the woman if she wanted me to help with her suntan oil, or I would have expected such a request simply because we were a man and a woman on a beach, in Mexico, with nothing better to do. That time floated out to sea on the tide that slapped the rim of the continent. I did not particularly regret its passing.

I had drifted into a steaming funk of idle humanity. I thought of nothing more than how I could get another beer without moving from the damp cushion of my beach chair.

I heard her say, "I'm a writer. Freelance, mostly. Articles for magazines, newspapers. What does it take to keep your man, and why would you want to? That kind of stuff."

I stirred and waved my hands at the blue sky, as though that would make me coherent.

I said, "You must be good if you can afford a place around here. Philip Coangelo had to invest his pension and make a killing on a string of juice bars all along the Baja coast for him to keep his condo."

"Oh, I do all right. And the house is shared by a bunch of us, so we split all the expense. I get away, so—I can think. I know it's trite, but I want to do something more serious than magazine fluff. You probably guessed that I'm trying to write a novel."

I hadn't guessed anything of the sort, but I did not let her know that. She must have sensed my hesitation, and misread my lack of a response.

3

"Please, don't laugh. I've got several chapters finished."

She abruptly sat up and reached for her beach bag. The gaily colored tote contained only one item, a stained and warped cardboard box that at one time had protected a ream of virgin typewriter paper. Rachel placed it in my hands and then dropped back on the blanket. I eased into my beach chair and turned my attention to the box.

"I've got a half-dozen copies of those, for people I meet who might give me a reaction. I like to know what people think about my book. Maybe you can read it and provide some feedback?"

A hint of emotion crept into her voice. Here was something that interested her.

"I'm not much of a reader."

"That's not good, and you, an educated man. When you want, come by and we can talk about my book. I mean it about my writing."

My nap never would return, and no good reason to be antisocial came to me. I decided that I should talk. I gave her too much detail about my situation back home—the trouble and how I ended up with a bum knee.

I explained how the state supreme court had only recently lifted its sanctions and permitted me to start my practice again, and I had tried to resurrect my legal career. Time worked against me, so I did not have a chance to rearrange all the pieces of my life before I had to dive back into the grind of trying to make it again as a once-suspended, charged-with-multiple-felonies, formerly-on-the-run, fugitive Chicano lawyer. I described the banal details of how I set up shop in a room in my house and hung my old office sign across my porch. I made much about a handful of acquaintances in the Hispanic Bar As-

4

sociation who tried to soothe their prickly consciences for running out on me when I needed their support by sending me some opportune referrals. A few quick fender-bender settlements with insurance companies, a couple of retainers from criminal defendant clients who were intrigued by the possibility of having the infamous Luis Montez represent them, and the always popular divorce clients, and I had almost regained my financial footing.

I told Rachel that for the span of several weeks I had been the focus of nasty newspaper headlines and TV investigative reporters. But I thought all that was behind me. I embellished the scene when I walked into a Denver courtroom to enter my appearance in a messy domestic squabble and Judge Garcia publicly welcomed me back. I was persuaded that I had a new lease on the last two decades or so of my income-earning years.

But my wounded body hadn't cooperated with my attempts at resurrecting the scattered remains of my career, and I had to rest. When I had a dead week of time, I made arrangements to accept Philip's long-standing offer of a place to chill.

"And here I am, and now I've met you."

Except for a grunt that I think was her way of acknowledging our newly established relationship, she did not react to my lengthy meandering down memory lane. There had been a glimmer of excitement when she had spoken about her writing, but that had quickly passed. The melancholy returned and with it our silence. We ignored each other for several minutes, and eventually she said, "I'll probably drift off for a nap. I was up late last night."

I collected my few items of beach paraphernalia and walked back to Coangelo's place.

The ocean rolled against my legs and the sand gave

way under my feet with each step. My knee worked extra hard. I had to stop several times because of the pain. I tried to think of other things.

I had arrived on the same night that Coangelo had left for a business meeting up north in the town of Tecate. Philip regularly conferred with his Mexican partners, the nominal owners of the juice bar chain. Among several words of caution, he had warned me about Rachel.

"There's a crazy group in the place next door. They call themselves artists, writers, you know. I think they're kooks. There's one, knowing you, you'll like her. Rachel. Cute, sexy. But out there, Louie. Be careful with her."

He was right. I liked her.

I calmed down over the next couple of days and almost put her out of my head. She did not make an appearance again, although I camped out on the beach each day for several hours, and, in the evenings, wandered conspicuously close to her house. There wasn't much activity at her place that I could see, and her effect on me gradually wore off. I decided I did not need any kooks. I needed rest.

Coangelo had filled his space with plenty of amenities: sauna, climate-controlled shower, superb sound system, beautiful view of the beach. I took advantage of them all in my efforts to resuscitate my body and my spirit.

The day before I was scheduled to leave, I filled the whirlpool one last time. The hot, foaming water relaxed my knee. My mind downshifted into semidrowsiness, my favorite state while in Mexico.

When I climbed out of the hot tub, I wrapped a beach towel around my waist. My stiff leg stretched along the cool tile of the floor as I sipped on a gin and tonic with a nice chunk of lime and examined Rachel's manuscript. I had set it aside and not bothered looking at it since she had given it to me. I undid the rubber band around the box and began to read. There were about two hundred typewritten pages and then several more of handwritten notes, drawings, figures, and strange symbols I couldn't decipher.

She had written about the killing of an innocent man in a serious case of mistaken identity, but no one, including the man's wife, suspected murder. The youngest daughter, only ten, presumably knew something, but, at least in the few pages I read, she wasn't talking. I skipped over the novel and tried to get a fix on the handwritten notes, but Rachel's flowery script made it difficult. I was losing interest when loud, insistent knocking saved me from an afternoon nap. A voice hollered through the walls of the condo.

"¡Señor Montez! ¡Señor Montez! ¡Abra la puerta! ¡Necesito hablar con usted, inmediatamente! Open up!"

I limped to the door. My knee felt stiff and weak. There was something about the tone of the guy's voice that I did not like, something too familiar.

"For God's sake, quit your pounding! What is it?"

He was tall and angular, dressed in Mexican peon clothes—white cotton pajamas held around his body with rough strands of rope—and I wasn't sure if he was Mexican, a well-tanned North American, or something else, maybe even Asian. His eyes had a squint, but I knew plenty of Chicanos who were more chino-looking than anything else, and the Mexican sun could wrinkle and squeeze the skin around a rhinoceros's eye, never mind the skin of a tourist from Detroit.

"Perdón. I am sorry to bother you. My name is Rudolfo Flores. I work for the people next door; I take care of their place. But they all seem to have left, without telling anyone they were leaving, without paying their bills, without paying me. And I had hoped that maybe you could take care of this."

"What? I don't understand. They left?"

"They owe large amounts of money at the restaurant, the market, the bar. They are all gone. The women, Kodiack the writer, that other man, Gulf. And we thought, that is, because you are also North American, and you knew the girl, that is, I've been sent by the *alcalde* to see if you know anything about them, where they might have gone?"

I did not want to get involved in anything even slightly off center. I wasn't in the mood for any new adventures.

"I'm sorry, but I don't actually know those people. I can't do anything about them. I'm sorry. Tell the *alcalde* that I can't do anything, that maybe when Mr. Coangelo returns, he might know something about them. But right now, I need to put some clothes on."

I shut the door in his worried face.

The next day, I flew back to Denver, the box with the manuscript taking up space in my bag because I did not know what else to do with it. I thought I'd call Coangelo later and ask him about the girl. Maybe he knew an address. I did not see Flores again, and the *alcalde* never took the time to drop by and introduce himself. When I landed in Denver, Rachel and her disappearing act and writing career were not priorities.

2

◆

Use it or lose it, Luis."

Not exactly young Dr. Kildare, but I got the idea. The good Doctor Webster had prescribed long walks, every day, if my knee was to have any future.

I worked out a regimen of physical exertion that Webster approved of, even though he was doubtful that I would keep with it. I'd start out from my office in midmorning, and make my way through the different Northside neighborhoods that surrounded the business intersection of Thirty-eighth Avenue and Federal Boulevard. Sometimes I'd make it back before noon, and sometimes I kept at it until I had to eat. On those energetic days, I'd grab a throat-scorching burrito from Chubby's at the distant east end of Thirty-eighth, or something kinder and gentler from the Taquería Pátzcuaro on Thirty-second, near my own digs, professional and household.

I grew up on Thirty-eighth, a straight shot of bruised houses hunkered against the traffic. It was a too-busy street that stretched across the heart of the Chicano community in Denver's northwest quadrant. Buildings that changed fronts as often as the calendar changed months struggled valiantly to add to the woeful tax base of my part of the city. Homes with small patches of lawn shared the avenue with fast-food joints, liquor stores, gas stations, and the imaginative hopes of eager, small-time entrepreneurs, the backbone of the U.S. economy, as my high-school social studies teacher once asserted.

If I wanted to, I could walk the several miles of Thirty-eighth from Sheridan to Lipan, and buy just about anything I might ever need: Italian sausage and pastries, a rebuilt carburetor for my gasping Bonneville, rebuilt boots from a *zapatero* from Zacatecas, a ride on a roller-coaster, a Big Mac or a Whopper or the Colonel's Extra Crispy, a miniskirt from Ropa Guapa for that someone special, life insurance, porno paperbacks in Spanish or English. The enterprising consumer could even shop around for the best deal on legal advice from a cluster of Chicano attorneys whose offices dotted Thirty-eighth with signs proudly displaying the Spanish surnames and the useful information that *Sí, se habla Español.*

There were a few drawbacks to using one of the city's main arteries as my exercise path. The avenue was noisy, and the pollution could lay a stubborn gray film of grit and grime on my all-season, never-need-pressing sport coats. Some of the young men who cruised its lanes were just obnoxious enough to keep me away. When a smart-ass pair of low-riding home-boys in a pretty, tricked-up black-and-orange minitruck with diminutive wheels sprayed me with what I hoped was water from a double-barreled water cannon, I gave up on using Thirty-eighth as my personal training center. I wandered the other streets of the Northside.

The seventy-year-old elms and the fifty-year-old houses eased me into the comfort zone that meant home. Often, the scenes were familiar and repetitive. I'd watch a pair of sweethearts from somewhere in Mexico where people dressed in cowboy hats and tight jeans, hugging and kissing while they washed the family station wagon; children chasing each other through alleys, laughing and crying until they collapsed in a cluttered yard; a friendly but mangy and thirsty black Chow who roamed the streets in search of a handout.

And then there were days when everything was different.

I had been back in Denver from my vacation for about a week. My walk had taken me past a pair of young girls in shorts and halter tops, smoking marijuana in what was supposed to be their front yard. They reminded me of many others, from years before, some of whom still lived in the area. These girls could have been their daughters. The hard-looking underage beauties swayed to loud Kid Frost and a Lighter Shade of Brown instead of James and Bobby Purify or El Chicano, but the idea was the same as when I had sat around a picnic table on stale summer afternoons with Gato, Frankie, and Chopper, chugging cheap red wine, getting a nasty headache, and having a good time. I played my role and did not ask the girls for a toke. Summer in the city, yes, oh yes.

A few minutes away I found the grand opening of the latest gift shop along West Thirty-second Avenue, east of the restaurants, closer to the bars and the really ugly apartment houses.

I strolled into an open doorway with a sign that said GIFTS—PARTY ITEMS—GROCERIES. A middle-aged man with prison tattoos stood behind a counter covered with balloons, cheap novelties, and a box of last year's baseball cards. Along the back wall a shelf swayed under new stock: cellophane bags of chile powder, cans of hominy, bags of beans, and other basics of a midweek supper.

"Come in, come in. What can I do for you?"

I assumed he spoke in English in deference to my tie and sweat-stained white shirt.

"I could use something to drink."

He almost ran to an old soda pop machine that chugged in the corner. He lifted the bent cover and extracted a wet, dripping can. I accepted it and handed him a dollar. I waved off his reluctant tender of change.

He said, "Let me introduce myself. Abel Tapia. This is my place. Tell your friends."

"Sure, Tapia. Good luck."

Tapia turned his attention to another man who had entered his store behind me. I had seen him earlier, up the street near the party girls, where I had thought he paid too much attention to my limp.

My first good look at him gave me a smiling, thin Chicano dressed in a very weary tan linen suit over a black T-shirt. Bare ankles showed beneath the cuffs of his pants, but the shoes were excellent—expensive-looking loafers with tassels and dingle-balls. They looked soft enough to take a nap in.

He walked straight to me and offered his hand.

"Mr. Montez? I've been looking for you. I went to your house, but it was empty. I wandered around until I saw you walking. I, uh, I followed you—hope you don't mind. I wasn't sure, you know."

I disposed of his handshake and waited for him to introduce himself. His nose was shiny, but his eyes were clear. He had a skin tone that used to be described as swart.

"Conrad Valdez. Nice to meet you. Here's my card. I've

heard so much about you. I wasn't sure what to expect."

His dark gray business card sported embossed blue lettering. CONRAD "RAD" VALDEZ was centered over a telephone number with an out-of-state area code. In smaller letters, the word *Investigations* politely sat in a bottom corner of the card.

"You're an investigator? What's this about? You trying to serve me with a summons?"

He laughed, politely, and shook his head.

"Now that's something a lawyer might say. No papers. I simply want to talk to you about a missing person. My client is a worried father. His daughter has been missing for several days. You might know something about the daughter's plans."

The way he said father and daughter made me jumpy as hell.

"Look, I haven't talked to anyone's daughter in months. Who the hell you looking for?"

He pulled a color photograph from his jacket pocket and held it up for me to see. Without looking, I knew who was in the picture.

"You were one of the last people to see her. Rachel Vargas."

I did not recognize the name and it must have been obvious on my face. Almost immediately, he said, "She probably introduced herself as Rachel Espinoza. You met in Mexico, Los Cabos, at Detective Coangelo's place. He confirmed that you were down there at the same time as Ms. Espinoza, and a very pissed-off Indian named Flores also confirmed that you spent some time with Ms. Espinoza. I hope you can shed some light on her disappearance. The father is very worried, as I mentioned."

I started to tell him that he should have had a more detailed conversation with my old pal Coangelo. The ex-cop had to know more about Ms. Espinoza than I. I was abruptly interrupted by a pair of guys in ski masks.

"Everyone on the floor! *Now*, motherfuckers! We'll blow you assholes away! On the fucking floor!"

One was much taller than the other, and they each carried semiautomatic handguns, but that was all I saw before the shorter one ran up to me and raised his gun to knock me to the floor, since I was a bit slow in doing what he had demanded. I ducked, instinctively, and pushed myself into his hips. From between his legs I watched Valdez slam the edge of his hand into the other guy's neck. Tall Bozo swirled and careened into the bags of chile and cans of hominy, and he was out. My guy was screaming and hollering, swinging his gun hand, but I had rolled out of the way. He ended on his knees, aiming his gun at the cowering store owner. Valdez jumped the holdup man from behind. His hands and legs moved quicker than I could put it together, but it meant that Short Bozo had been smashed a dozen or so times with hammer blows on all parts of his body. Short Bozo groaned, twisted into a ball, and collapsed on top of his buddy.

The sudden silence in the store did not last long. We were surrounded by a mad rush of excited neighborhood kids who had seen the aborted stickup from the street. They stood around us, glaring at the inert robbers and, in a frantic mix of Spanish and English, noisily admired the Chicano PI with the fists of stone and the wrinkled clothes. Another Northside legend.

Rad was very good with the cops who roared up to the storefront with sirens wailing and guns drawn. He explained in detail what had happened, and, for once, I did not have to try to squirm out of the suspicious assumptions of crime-scene officers. He spoke their language and shared their attitude about the hapless pair of outlaws who finally woke up when their wrists were fitted with handcuffs. Tapia bubbled with gratitude.

I was busy with my own project, anyway. My knee had locked when I rolled into the screaming robber and I had managed to con some pain relievers from the ambulance driver who had responded to the 911 call about a shooting.

Eventually we landed in front of a couple of jalapeño cheeseburgers at the Denver Bar and Grill. I figured I owed him dinner, such as it was. He was reluctant to take me up on my food recommendation.

"I don't eat much chile," he explained.

"I think you can handle it. You just kicked the asses of two wannabes. How tough can a hamburger be?"

He shrugged and went along with me. I commented on his demonstrated abilities with his fists and feet.

"I thought kung fu tricks were for the movies. I've never seen anything like that."

His lips curled into a smile and it was obvious that he was proud of the impression he had made. He liked to smile.

"It's not kung fu. Bit of judo, karate, this and that. My stepfather got me into martial arts when I was eight years old, and I stayed with it through the army. People think because I'm an investigator that I'm always using gadgets and tricks, but they really don't come up that often. And when I need my tricks, like you called them, it's usually for stupid assholes like those two at the store, not against anyone who knows what he's doing. Are Denver hoods all like that, or did we just run up against the bottom of the barrel? There couldn't have been more than five bucks in the cash register. Now they're facing twenty to forty."

He shook his head in disgust, or pity, and turned his attention to the food. A line of sweat framed his lips, and the shiny nose reflected the Denver's old-fashioned neon lighting.

"Nice place," he mumbled. His head swayed in time to the beat of "Duke of Earl." A bigger smile. "Great juke-box."

He looked a few years younger than the twenty-eight or so that I calculated he must have reached in order to accommodate a stint in the service and the setting up of his own business. That meant that he had been born when I was in high school. I copped a bit of condescension about his relative youth. What did he know? What could he know? But I kept it to myself. I did not pop-quiz him about the Chicano Movement, or ask for the real name of the leader of Question Mark and the Mysterians, or try for a historical perspective on the *Adelitas*. Maybe he knew, and maybe not, and maybe he didn't even care.

"Look, uh, Rad, what is this about Rachel Espinoza? I told you everything I know about her, and a couple of things I guessed about. She looked fine when I saw her. Fine."

He grinned again as though he could read between the lines of my words.

"But I didn't really know her, and I saw her only that one time. Your dramatic albeit timely appearance here in Denver raises more questions than answers. Like, Who's the old man who can afford to send a private detective all around the Southwest in search of a daughter who, from what I saw, really didn't need any looking after? If there was ever a young lady who could take care of herself, Rachel is that girl. I find it a little difficult to believe that Daddy hasn't been through this before. And I'd probably bet and give you odds that she's always managed to turn up, just in time for her allowance."

His bright grin faded.

"The old man, Montez, is my client, and that's all you need to know. Whatever you think about Ms. Espinoza, she is a missing person, and I haven't found her, yet. But her trail led me straight to you, and that means that I have to get what I can from you, learn everything that you know about her, everything that you're keeping from me, even if you don't realize it yourself, and then I'll move on, until I do find her. Which I will, Montez. Guaranteed. I know my job. I'm good at it. And I'm not as young as you think."

His face muscles had tensed, and his right hand rigidly clutched a napkin. He finished off his beer. I did not want to see him use his feet and elbows again, especially up against the side of my head. But one of his buttons had been pushed, and it was another good bet that the particular button's name was Rachel.

Carla the bartender/waitress/cook sashayed to our table with a pair of cold beers. She knew the effect of her homemade jalapeño cheese and had calculated the exact minute when we would need refills.

I toyed with the idea of talking about the white bikini. I threw that bikini in the air, watched it tumble in the Mexican sky, saw it float on warm Pacific waters, and I let it lie there. Rad and I could get to that later.

3

———◆———

It never fails, Louie. This guy won't give up. He's not sat-isfied that he's ruined me, now he's got to crap all over any kind of dignity I might have left. He's pushing me, hard, and if he doesn't stop, I'll take care of him. I swear. I'll hurt the little foreigner if I have to."

"Easy, Wilson, easy. Don't do anything crazy. He can't mess with you since your bankruptcy. There's an auto-matic stay on your creditors who might try to collect their debts. I went through this with you before we filed your bankruptcy petition. You were at the end of your finan-cial rope. The heat had to ease up so you could get some breathing room, a second chance. It's your constitutional right, the American way. You shed your bills, your cred-itors, and stay in business. And this guy, Kopinski, he's not even a business debt. It was a personal loan, the least secured. He's gone, disappeared into the bad debt bad-lands, and, like the song goes, he can't touch you."

Wilson Lopez shrugged his round shoulders and

shook his bald head. His nickname was Weeds. Something about where his buddies found him one summer night, so many years ago, curled up like a baby lamb, butt naked and disoriented. I never tried to find out more about his youth.

Lopez had come to me as a referral from Donna Gallegos, the longtime lady friend and business partner of Cool Cal, one of the group of pals who had bestowed the nickname Weeds on my client. The referral was made on behalf of Cool Cal, but I took on Lopez's problems as a favor to Donna, one of the more interesting people ever to come out of the Globeville neighborhood.

"Oh yeah? Then how does he get away with this?"

He held up the three-by-four-foot piece of cardboard he had carried with him into the extra bedroom that now served as my office. The sign was purple with lime green lettering—garish and brutal.

WILSON LOPEZ—DEADBEAT!
FILED BANKRUPTCY AND RAN OUT ON HIS DEBTS!
WARNING, LOSER AND CHISELER ON THIS BLOCK!
THIS IS A PUBLIC SERVICE ANNOUNCEMENT!

"Ouch. Are there any more of these?"

Wilson was so upset he could barely speak.

"All over the fucking street! Up and down my block! On trees, stuck in empty lots, on fences. Some of my neighbors let Kopinski plant these pieces of shit in their yards. I can't show my face on my own porch! And that ain't all. He leaves messages, or he has his ugly crone of a wife leave them. On our own phone we have to listen to him sputter about us being deadbeats, and that we better pay up. Says that he's not going to lay off until we pay.

All for a measly ten grand! You got to do something about this, Louie. 'Cause if you don't, sure as hell I'm going to! Sure as hell!"

I wanted to explain that the legal system, the damn judicial *process*, for crying out loud, was supposed to allow citizens the opportunity to resolve disputes without resorting to violence. Sue the bastards, not shoot the bastards. But Wilson's face was puffy and red and I feared he might explode if I gave him one of my lawyer-like speeches. I had just arranged my makeshift office and I did not want to have to clean up anything that Wilson might leave in the wake of his terrible need to stop the torment inflicted by the hardheaded, and just as hot-headed, Albert Kopinski.

"It's okay, Wilson. We can do something about it. The automatic stay ought to be enough to cite Kopinski for contempt. I'll ask the court for a restraining order to prevent this kind of stuff." I disdainfully waved my pen at the sign. "We'll hit him for your fees and costs, ask the court to keep him on a tight leash. In fact, I should call him up, maybe pay him a visit, see if I can't persuade him that it's in his best interests to get out of the sign-making business."

"You do what you have to, Montez. But I know Kopinski, known him for years. He was a guest at my oldest daughter's wedding, got stupid drunk, and I took him home. We used to be friends. But he's always been a stubborn son of a bitch. He's some kind of Romanian or Slavic or one of those European races. God, do I regret the day I let him talk me into taking his damn money. Ain't that rich? He was going to give me the ten thousand, and I'm the one who insisted it should be a loan. And, now, here we are . . . damn!"

"The only thing, well, the only problem might be . . ."

"What? What now?"

"You know, there is a thing called freedom of speech. And the bankruptcy stay might not apply to what he's doing. He's not, strictly speaking, collecting on a debt, you know what I mean?"

His face darkened to the purple hue of the sign. I backtracked before I had to wipe bits and pieces of his forehead off my freshly painted walls.

"But I'll work on it. It'll be all right. Please, leave it to me. Don't do anything until you hear from me. Is that clear?"

"Take care of it, Louie. Or I will."

We left it at that.

I kept myself occupied for what was left of the afternoon by working on the paperwork and research I would need for Lopez. I found a couple of cases with similar facts from other bankruptcy courts. They went both ways—one judge concerned about free speech and greatly expanding the court's limited jurisdiction, and another judge upset about the manipulation of his order that had restricted what creditors could do to one of the court's protected debtors. I thought that George Lowell, the judge who had been assigned to *In Re: Lopez,* wouldn't look too kindly on Albert Kopinski's creative postpetition maneuvers, even if there was a Bill of Rights loophole. To spur the judge on, I added to my motion the fact that Kopinski had tied his name calling and not-so-subtle threats to payment of the bill, at least according to what my client told me about the phone calls. Now that sounded like bill collection activity.

I hammered Kopinski for all I was worth in the motion for a contempt citation, then turned to my plans for the evening.

I picked up Rad at his hotel a few hours after I had nuked a frozen, but healthy, packaged dinner. I drove the sensible, late-model compact that I believed had finally solved my transportation problems. Nothing fancy, and so not too expensive to repair, and like nothing that I had collected over the years that tended to resemble a machine for spraying insect plagues. The monthly payments were a stretch, but I managed them. Since it was a lease arrangement, I did not have to come up with a down payment of any consequence. My recent trouble had forced me to dispose of my cranky sports car and I had finally retired my 1975 Bonneville Brougham to the safety and comfort of my father's garage.

Valdez and I had become something of an item. We spent time with each other for our own separate reasons. Rad had talked himself into believing that I had more to reveal about Rachel Espinoza, and he hung around like a hungry, lost puppy. From my perspective, Rad Valdez did not know much about Denver and even less about the Denver Chicano community, and I thought some cultural exposure would do him good.

A rhinestone sparkled from his left earlobe and his hair looked freshly trimmed. He had on a clean white polo shirt, but his pants overwhelmed the attempt at neatness—they were the same bedraggled pair he had on when we had first met and he had given the Northside a quick lesson in self-defense.

"Where did you say this is, what did you call it, *tertulia?*"

"Back room of a bookstore and coffee shop. Nothing

formal, just a handful of writers, musicians, you know. They sit around and intellectualize about being artists. I've known some of them for years, and they tolerate me because I act like I'm impressed."

"Your idea of fun?"

"It's all right. And if you get bored, we can do something else. Promise. Chicano honor."

I raised my open hand to emphasize my sincerity, but his mind was elsewhere, probably with Rachel on a beach of their own.

The Keyhole had been around for a couple of decades, but the small bookshop had changed hands so many times over the years that no one remembered why it had that name. I knew it as the 'Hole; very few people referred to it as the Keyhole anymore. As a college student home for summer break, I had watched *teatros* on a stage that now served as the main area of the coffee shop where tables and chairs were scattered among newspapers and magazines. For a few months, way back when, the place had been the headquarters for the Socialist Workers Party, when that Trotskyite conglomeration had made organizing the "national minorities" a priority. That did not work. The SWP minions hurriedly removed their files and posters after one of their new recruits punched out the shaggy-haired director and tried to teach his young assistant, fresh from an East Coast all-girls school, how to do the forbidden horizontal bop. As I passed on this bit of historical color to Rad, I felt like a real old-timer. Almost every street in northern Denver—hell, almost every building—represented a piece of my past.

Rad needed some explanation about the SWP, and why they would be "organizing" Chicanos. I did what I could and laid on him my five-minute condensation of fifteen years of stale politics and moldy movement mementos.

The 'Hole filled a hole in the landscape of a street that did not go anywhere. Two rather neat houses shared the curb on either side of the bookstore, and it could have been someone's home, too, if that particular someone liked a color scheme of green, black, and brown. Somewhere in its history, the 'Hole had been painted with colors that represented the New Africa, or maybe it was the New Earth, something New—I was never sure. A yellowed, stained sign in a window displayed only the words CAFE Y LIBROS.

Rad's smile had taken root on his face and grew as we approached the 'Hole.

"Who would try to keep a business going in this cul-de-sac? And why?"

"Around here it's called a dead end. Donna Gallegos owns the place. Nice lady, early forties. She grew up in these streets and bought the building when she got the chance. She's trying to bring something to the community, give the neighborhood a chance, maybe a chance just to think, if that's what they need. Not much time for thinking around here. This part of Denver is called Globeville, but the world is pretty small for most of these folks. So Donna does what she can. She runs it with her boyfriend Cool Cal."

"Cool Cal? You actually refer to someone as Cool Cal? Why?"

"Man, I don't know. He's been Cool Cal forever, since he was a kid. Anytime anyone says his name, it's always Cool Cal. Not Cal, Calvin, or Calcutta. Cool Cal. I don't even know his last name."

Rad held up his hands in mock surrender to my defensiveness.

"It's okay with me, Louie. This is your town, your friends."

I parked the car and we walked to the back of the house. A bare bulb sprayed light across the entrance, and a bell jingled when we opened the door. The room was stuffy and hot. Packed bookshelves leaned against the walls. The smell of freshly brewed coffee mixed with cigarette smoke and the melodious strumming of a guitar. A dozen people sat in small groups around the main room, on wicker chairs and lumpy sofas, drinking coffee, talking to each other with the intensity of United Nations delegates. I knew most of them, if not well at least by reputation. Poets joked with a few members of the band Cariño Nuevo, while a pair of muralists sparred academically with a young student who espoused the benefits of computer art.

Donna greeted me with a hug.

"Primo. How's the knee?" She did not wait for an answer. "You're looking good. And this young man, looking even better. Must be the guy who wiped out the Torres brothers. You're famous, kid."

She wrapped her arms around Rad and snuggled his head into the comfort of her bosom. He looked to me for direction.

"Easy, Donna. Rad here might wet his pants if you keep squeezing him like that."

She laughed, released him, and found us a couple of chairs.

Donna whispered in my ear while Rad tried to make himself comfortable.

"He's been asking about you all over the Northside. Cool Cal says your new friend's interested in info about a young woman, some dolly whose bones you bounced in Mexico. Thought you should know."

Rad noticed the whispering and asked, "You're related? Cousins, right?"

"No, no. She calls everyone *primo*. It's just her way."

In a few minutes Rad had a glass of Donna's version of iced coffee while I chugged on lemonade. Sweat dribbled down my back even though I had discarded my tie and coat back in the car. A steady hum vibrated through the place. We were surrounded by voices, music, the growl of the espresso machine, and a couple of clanging fans that Donna had set near the doorway.

"Hey, Louie, this your private dick?"

"You couldn't resist? Come up with something original, Bobby. You're a poet, right? Be poetic."

Bobby Baca laughed and sat next to Rad. Baca had published a half-dozen chapbooks, and, when he wasn't repairing TVs and VCRs out of his garage, he edited *The Shiv,* a literary magazine that featured inner-city writers but couldn't live up to promises to come out on a quarterly basis. His most resonant claim to fame was that early in his writing years he had penned the epic song about Chicano resistance, "Pachuco, Low Rider, Xicano." It had captured the minds, hearts, and sentiment of young militants across the Southwest in 1968, and secured his place in the mythology of the oppressed. Even I had sung the words of what came to be called "The Pachuco Song." I had felt the tugging at my nationalistic heart inspired by the song's emotional appeal for justice and equality against the overpowering odds of racism and hatred. Baca's lyrics had been the anthem of the Aztlán nation. I introduced him to Rad, and soon the others in the room made their way to our corner.

Indeed, Rad was famous. His expert handling of the bungled holdup had made the evening news and the next day's newspapers. In honor of his presence, Baca announced that his latest work in progress would have a few lines about Rad's Righteous Rescue.

I interrupted before Baca could launch into his poem.

"Don't take it seriously, Rad. They'll get tired of pimping you in a few minutes."

"I like it, Louie. Hell, he can write a book if he wants."

The rangy, dark-haired woman who had been picking the guitar eased onto the sofa arm next to Rad. She introduced herself, vigorously pumped Rad's hand, and took over the conversation.

"Hell yes! A novel! The young man deserves his own novel. Who will be the first to write a novel about this brave and handsome private eye? A movement mystery, a lurid Latino hard-boiled paperback, all about the crime investigator with lightning fists and flashing feet, and eyes that could melt the heart of any dragon lady!"

She rubbed Rad's shoulders. He shriveled in embarrassment. Baca roared with laughter, and some of the others chuckled. Rad's smile popped back on his face.

I slapped his knee.

"Don't worry, *joven,* she's spoken for. You'd have to be a very special person to take on Charlotte Garcia."

He looked relieved.

Bobby and Charlotte began a debate about Chicano mysteries. Bobby wanted to know why Charlotte thought they had to be political.

She had a quick and ready rejoinder.

"Because Chicanas and Chicanos live political lives. We can't escape it, whether we're running for City Council or trying to get decent teachers in the schools, or even just looking for a good price on a used car. It's all political, Bobby. Even a social nihilist like you knows that."

"No way, José, I mean, Josie. *La llorona* ain't political. *Curanderas* and *brujas*—not political."

Charlotte wouldn't hear it.

"Of course they are! How can you say that? But anyway, those aren't mysteries like I was thinking about. Those are the supernatural, the spirit world. I mean mysteries, man. What really happened to *Los Seis*? Who did the Biltmore? Who set up Ricardo Falcon or a hundred other martyrs to *la causa*? What was Ruben Salazar doing in the Silver Dollar Cafe? Where's Zeta? Those are mysteries, man, and political from the jump. As political as you can get. *¿Verdad,* Louie?"

"Don't drag me into your perpetual argument. Ask Rad here what he thinks about your mysteries. But I need to warn you, he doesn't have a good foundation in Chicano history. You might have to explain what and who you're talking about."

Rad had latched onto Charlotte's words, and he took his opportunity to ask her some questions.

"Yeah, Louie's right. I don't know too much about the yorona, or those other people. But that one name, Zeta. Is that the lawyer, Oscar Acosta?"

Charlotte nodded her head approvingly.

"Hear that? Our young investigator here does know something about the history of his people. Zeta and Oscar Acosta, one and the same. The first, and some would say, the only real Chicano lawyer. The Brown Buffalo himself. Novelist, a radical from the old, old movement, and then that gonzo guy, Thompson, made him famous when he wrote about Las Vegas and the wild drug days. Zeta, a real hero for all of us. A pig of course—he had no respect for women. And some think he was a provocateur, and a drug dealer. Of course he was called a sellout too, but then who among us is ever really Chicano enough? But, Oscar Acosta was a damn good writer."

Bobby chimed in.

"Even I have to agree with that. Young man, Mr. Investigator, you have to read *The Autobiography of a Brown Buffalo* and *The Revolt of the Cockroach People.* How can any Chicano go through life, and have even a tiny clue, without reading the books of Oscar Acosta?"

"Uh, right. I'll pick them up, next chance. But, tell me, what do you think happened to Acosta? What's the big mystery?"

Charlotte took the cue.

"The story, such as it is, is simple. He vanished. Disappeared in nineteen seventy-four, off the coast of Mazatlán. He'd been kicking back, here in Colorado, up in the mountains. He was trying to get it together. It had turned very heavy for him. He'd run for sheriff of L.A., and had his life threatened. He'd defended people accused of inciting the riot at the Chicano Moratorium, and had his life threatened. He wrote books about real Chicanas and Chicanos, street people and wild nights, about the movement, not the tortillas-and-beans books that college professors call Chicana/Chicano literature. It was a crazy, out-there lifestyle. He left our mountains and turned up south of the border. One day he took off in a small boat. He told everyone, including his family, that he was sailing back to the States. He never made it, and no one ever heard from him again. Officially, that is. He's been sighted, of course, in Mexico and Cuba, East L.A., and the Conjunto Festival in San Antonio."

Baca added, "And with Elvis, using TVs for target practice on the lawn of Graceland. Don't forget that, Charlotte."

She slugged his arm.

"Don't fuck around, Bobby. I'm trying to be serious here."

Rad also was serious.

"But you said that's the official story. What's the unofficial line?"

Charlotte loved it.

"My own opinion, Mr. Beautiful Eyes, is that Acosta was hit by the feds—CIA, FBI, major *marranos*. There was a federal program of counterintelligence against progressive groups and progressive leaders. Acosta's name came up on the list and he bought it. Either that, or . . ."

Even I had been drawn in by the tone and tempo of her voice.

"Or what, Charlotte? Damn!"

"Or he just had enough, and he boogied for some South Pacific island, where's he's still doing massive quantities of whatever he wants and no one gives him heat about anything. Take your pick."

Baca roared. "It could happen! And dear Charlotte here will milk the legend of Oscar Acosta for whatever it's worth. *Mujer,* I love you."

He reached for her and gave her a loud stage kiss on her forehead. She wiped the spot where his lips had lingered and wrinkled her face in disgust.

It was a good time to investigate the investigator.

"Why the sudden curiosity in Zeta, Rad? I thought you immune to Chicanismo in general, and Chicano myths in particular."

"Don't rag on me so much, Louie. I'm not that much of a lost case. But to tell you the truth, I'm only doing my job. It's all part of finding Rachel Espinoza."

"What the hell could Oscar Acosta have had to do with that nymphet? You lost me, Rad. Unless it's the writing angle."

"It's just that, well, you see, it's like this. According to her friends back in Los Angeles, and the people she stayed with in Mexico, Rachel Espinoza claimed for the past year or so that she was Oscar Acosta's daughter."

Charlotte and Bobby stopped their arguing and turned their attention to Rad.

I said, "Are you serious? It must be a joke, a con."

"I'm just telling you what I found out. She said she spent time with Acosta when she was a kid. The really trippy part is that she told her friends that she had talked with him, like recently, and she would soon be with him. Somehow, she had found him or he had found her. Her plan was for her to spend time with her long-lost father. Then she vanished, Louie. Disappeared right after she met you."

Charlotte and Bobby stared at the two of us. They were about to say something. I was about to ask about Rad's client, whom I thought he had said was Rachel's father. None of us got the chance.

The front window shattered, the old yellow sign fluttered in the air, and something hard landed on the creaky wooden floor. A loud crash made me twitch in my chair as if I had stuck my thumb in a wall socket. I smelled gasoline, and smoke, and then, before any of us could do anything about it, fire streamed in all directions along the floor. In seconds, the front part of the building was engulfed in flames.

Donna Gallegos screamed. Bobby Baca grabbed her around her waist and rushed her through the back door. Billows of smoke surrounded us as the books, magazines, and newspapers fed the fire. Everyone ran to the back door but there was no way we could all rush to the outside at once.

I lifted the first heavy object my hands latched onto. It was one of Donna's secondhand chairs. Smoke and heat urged me to act. Rad was herding people through the door, but their escape took too much time. I hurled the chair through a window. The glass cracked in a thousand pieces and the entire frame crumbled. Air rushed in and fanned the fire behind us, but now we had another exit.

I helped somebody crawl to safety, and then I was out in the yard. We ran from the 'Hole, looking for cover from the small explosions that shattered the building. We watched it burn to the ground, then stood back when the fire truck showed up and the firemen saved the neighboring houses by dousing them with water and smothering the remains of the 'Hole.

Rad had guided a few coughing and gagging people. He stood next to me. Long black smears of charcoal smudged his shirt, and it was impossible to recognize its original color. From his shoulders and hair, wisps of smoke curled into the night sky.

"Did everyone get out?"

I shrugged.

"I think so but I can't be sure. It all happened so quick. There's Donna and Bobby, with the others. She looks like she's going to pass out. Poor woman. Her whole life, up in smoke in just a few minutes. Christ!"

"Luis, wait. How about Charlotte? Do you see her? What happened to her?"

4

At eight in the morning, the best I could do for Bonnie Collins was a cup of coffee. Charlotte's partner of more than a decade looked beaten down. I hoped she hadn't fallen back into old habits. Before she and Charlotte had settled into domestic stability, Bonnie had traversed the rough, tough road of alcohol, drugs, and pain that she passed off as sex. I wanted her to maintain, to stick and stay, for Charlotte's memory if for nothing else. But, as I watched her drawn, taut face, I knew that I would have self-destructed the night of the fire if it had been my lover, my friend and savior, who had been trapped while trying to smother the deadly mix of gasoline, a makeshift wick made from a burning rag, and shards of a broken bottle.

"I wish there was something I could say or do, Bonnie. Charlotte was one in a million, very special. I thought she was a great writer, and an even better person. I'm sorry."

"Thank you, Louie. She always said you were fair. You've already done so much. Arranging for the service and all. And, you know, I think, at least I hope, that there is something else you can do. If you think you can."

"I'll give it a shot. What is it?"

Her tired, red eyes wandered across the wall behind me. It couldn't have been easy for her to talk about Charlotte. In the early morning light filtered through half-open blinds, she seemed to have an abundance of gray hair that I had never noticed before.

"I guess it's because you're a lawyer. You have access to people and places that I could never get to. The police have already come to a conclusion about what happened. They think it was a bunch of kids who've been vandalizing the neighborhood. Typical gang-banger stuff. They can't prove it, of course. They're trying to pressure some of the younger boys. They told me that sooner or later one of them would crack and give up the names of those who were involved. But I can't believe it, Louie. I know some of those kids. Charlotte knew them a lot better. They're troublemakers, sure, but their thing is graffiti, fights with other kids. That kind of stuff. They don't set fires. They don't burn just for the hell of it. They had no motivation to throw a Molotov into the Keyhole. None at all!"

I had heard the police theory, and the Globeville rumors, and I wasn't as sure as Bonnie that the cops were on the wrong track. For one thing, the "kids" were more than just "troublemakers." I had represented at least one of the bunch, and a pair of the older ones had already served time at the Lookout Mountain School for Boys and were obviously on their way to the Buena Vista Reformatory. They were into drugs, assaults, and car thefts. Personally, I would cross the street if I ran into them on one of the blocks they patrolled. But that wasn't the only justification for trusting the line of the police investigation.

"The police did a check on everyone who had any connection to the 'Hole, from Donna and Cool Cal to me and Rad. The crowd that night probably wouldn't ever get invited to the policemen's ball, but no one stuck out as an obvious target of a firebomb. In fact, I was the shadiest guy in the place, but my last real enemy got blown away almost a year ago. Nobody knows Rad in Denver, except for the Torres brothers, and they were locked up and still nursing their bruises from the beating he gave them. Donna and Cool Cal don't have enemies, not even creditors. And insurance couldn't have been the provocation—they didn't have any."

Bonnie listened to me but she did not react. I tried something else.

"And another thing. Charlotte died because she was trapped trying to save the rest of us. She was fighting the fire, or at least slowing it down enough so that we had time to get out. The arsonist couldn't have counted on that. It was too random, too haphazard. Even if it wasn't the particular kids that the cops have singled out, it had to be someone like them—a crazy thrill-seeker who thought a fire would be fun. I think that's the way it went down, Bonnie. I really do."

"It sounds logical, Louie. But it doesn't feel right. I guess—I hoped—oh, I don't know. To lose Charlotte, for no damn reason. It's, it's . . ."

She couldn't finish. She broke down and cried into a handkerchief she had been squeezing and rolling in her hands.

I pushed a box of tissues in her direction.

"I know, I know. Charlotte deserved more. Bobby Baca and some of the others are working on something for her.

37

They're planning to publish a collection of her stories, poems, and songs. I think Bobby will do a nice job."

"Yes. I suppose he will."

She regained her balance, but said nothing else. We both sat in silence for a few minutes. Finally, with a stomach full of doubt, I offered what I could.

"Look, maybe there is more to it. I'll keep my ears open, ask around. I know enough cops and suspects, including these kids, that I should hear something."

She hesitated, then nodded. There had to be something else.

"We've got Rad, the professional investigator. He'll pitch in, for as long as he's around Denver. Let's see what he turns up. We'll check it out, Bonnie. I promise."

Albert Kopinski gripped the handle of a socket wrench between pudgy, grease-stained fingers. More grease and drops of oil accented his thinning, gray-and-brown crew-cut hair and the lenses of his black horn-rimmed glasses.

Kopinski had worked long hours at the Double K Garage six days and many nights of the week for more than twenty years. The indelible marks of a mechanic—grease and oil—had saturated his skin and work clothes. He owned the business and he loved it. Lopez had told me that Kopinski often slept in the garage. He laughed when he let me in on one of the confidences the two had shared when they had been friends: "Kopinski thinks it's work to go home to his wife."

When I had called to set up our meeting, my client's nemesis had reluctantly agreed only because, as he said, "Maybe there's a chance some decency can be forced down Weeds's throat." We were alone in the garage except for the two lube jobs and one U-joint replacement that sat on the hydraulic racks. Kopinski's mechanic had taken off for the day. In the background, easy listening music competed with the sounds of evening rush-hour traffic on Thirty-eighth.

I had walked to his place of business from my place of business, my house, and the walk had taken twenty minutes. My knee was tired and I could have used a drink of water, but Kopinski and I did not waste time with social pleasantries.

"So, when is Lopez paying the money he owes? That's all I want to hear about. I don't have time for a fast-talking lawyer who's trying to cover for that deadbeat. He owes ten thousand dollars, not counting interest. He's owed it for three years. I want it. You got the money, lawyer?"

"I'm here to explain a few things, Mr. Kopinski, in case it wasn't clear. Mr. Lopez's bankruptcy protects him from creditors. That's the law. In your case, it means that the debt has been discharged and you have to stop—"

"The hell you say! Discharged my ass! I don't care what no limp-dicked judge put down in no piece of paper, and I don't care what no lawyer's got to say about his so-called rights. What about *my* fucking rights? What about what's right? That money saved Weeds's worthless life. It kept him from getting killed. And he knows it. If he isn't man enough to pay, then I'm going to broadcast it to all the world, to everyone, so that everyone will know just what kind of man he is."

He studied the wrench and I hoped he wasn't measuring it against the size of my skull. I started to say something but he interrupted.

"But that's what I should expect. He doesn't have the balls to come here and tell me himself. He sends his errand boy. Well, since you're the messenger, take this message back to Lopez."

He stepped forward, holding the wrench high, and I stepped backward, up against the emissions inspection machine.

"Back off, Kopinski. I'm here for your own good. You're violating a federal bankruptcy court order, and I will have it enforced, by the cops if I have to. The judge—"

"Fuck the judge! And fuck your bankruptcy court! You tell Lopez that if my money isn't in my hands by the end of this week, our mutual friend will call on him. Tell him, Mr. Lawyer. Now get the hell out of my place before I use this wrench on your damn head."

He pounded the wrench into the palm of his free hand. I inched around the emissions machine and debated picking up a tire iron that lay at my feet. His eyes followed mine and he tensed when he realized what I was thinking.

I moved past the tire iron.

"You're making a mistake, Kopinski. I'd hoped we could do something positive. Now this is headed back to court, and you will have to answer to Judge Lowell. You can rely on that."

"Get the fuck out!"

I left him at the entrance to his garage bay, shaking his head, savagely smashing the wrench into his hand, and swearing at the American legal system, judges, and the deadbeat Wilson Lopez. I limped out of the range of his voice as he started in on lawyers.

5

◆

A brass lamp with a loose and shaky green glass shade offered the only illumination, and that was limited to a bright circle of light centered on the middle of my desk. Canadian whiskey and ice occasionally clinked together in a sweaty glass near my hand. A fan moved the warm air over my head and up against the wall. I absentmindedly rubbed my knee, a habit I had picked up over the past several months.

The Autobiography of a Brown Buffalo lay open before me in the circle of light, the paperback torn and bent. I hadn't looked at it for years but now I read pages from it again, searching in vain for the clue that would link Zeta and the vanished Rachel Espinoza.

If I believed every word in the book, Acosta was a madman and a saint. His voracious appetite for life took him into worlds of excess—drugs, alcohol, gluttony—yet also made him a harsh but accurate prophet of a country torn apart by racism and the violent, if doomed, outrage of the previously humiliated, exploited, and oppressed. Published in 1972, the book covered the late sixties and the changes Acosta went through as his consciousness awoke and liberated itself, similar to what youth around the world were trying to do in those same years.

His lifestyle easily could have generated unofficial offspring, but the tone of his book made me believe that if the fact of an extra daughter was true, it would have been revealed in his writing. Zeta's art did not come from a soul that kept secrets about itself.

Acosta would have been sixty years old if he had survived his ocean excursion. I thought of the possibilities. Maybe he would have stayed in politics and ended up in the same place as so many others from that era: arguing for a piece of the pie for his constituents to bored and sullen members of the opposition party, playing the politics game with all of its inherent compromises and inadequacies, and positioning for sound-bite exposure on the news. Maybe he would have kept at his writing and produced overwhelming literature about culture, race, love, and hate. Or—and this option seemed more in character with the man I knew only from his books—after his eventual best-seller he would have moved to Aspen and hobnobbed with the glitterati between deadlines for the national magazine catering to the so-called new and emerging Hispanic market. But the vision I enjoyed most was one of Oscar Zeta Acosta hosting his own talk show, bobbing and weaving with his guests and, eventually, blistering and embarrassing everyone from the chief of the Los Angeles Police Department to the latest sex-toy pop singer. Now that was an Oscar Acosta I could appreciate.

I eased back into my old leather chair and played the

ice in my drink against my lips. Rad and Rachel and Zeta—a pair of unlikely heroes and a young woman about whom I knew very little except that she heated up a Mexican beach in a special way. I touch-toned the number for Rad's hotel and asked for his room.

"Hello, Rad. I think we should talk, bud. For Bonnie Collins. We have to do something about figuring out the fire at the 'Hole. But we should talk anyway. We have more to tell each other about Rachel."

Without additional urging, he agreed to meet me at my house in half an hour.

"She was adopted by Oscar and Lucille Vargas when she was three. Up until that time she had been a ward of the State of California, in and out of hospitals and foster homes. The Vargas family is one of the old-line families, original *Californios*—they trace their lineage straight back to the Spanish governors in the days of Padre Serra, the missions, and Zorro, I guess."

Rad and I had downed a glass each of the smooth whiskey. In return for my promise of complete candor about Rachel, he had opened up with his own story. He sat across the desk in the half-light, an occasional twinkle bouncing from his earring, while I eased deeper into my stiff rotating chair. I stretched my leg and tried to be comfortable.

He pulled a thin metallic case from his leather briefcase and unlocked it.

"Is that one of those laptop computers?"

"Yeah. I keep my notes and research on it. Everything that I'm working on, actually."

The room was semidark, for no particular reason. It matched my mood, if nothing else, and Rad did not complain, even though he had to squint at his computer screen under the glare of my rickety lamp.

"You need an outlet?"

"No thanks. Batteries keep it humming."

Of course. Rad was nothing if not up-to-date. Self-consciously I moved a couple of writing pads that I had sitting on my desk. Written notes suddenly struck me as inefficient.

He pushed the right buttons on his keyboard and after a few seconds of whirs and clicks, and a quick glance at his screen, he said, "There's not much I've learned about her before the adoption. The social services file was confidential, but I knew somebody who knew somebody—you know how it is. And certain records are public—there's all kinds of information sitting at credit bureaus, banks, motor vehicle departments, court-houses. The caseworker's report says that her mother, Elena Satana, was about nineteen when she was rushed into the county hospital in Los Angeles, hemorrhaging and in shock. Satana died during childbirth, and no one ever claimed the body."

He moved his fingers and his machine made a soft purring sound. His eyes moved back and forth as he scrolled pages in random order to fill in holes in his story. As I listened, I changed my concept of what made a private investigator. The investigators I did business with were run-of-the-mill errand boys for the most part. They served subpoenas, obtained driving or criminal records, interviewed names on my witness list, and reduced the interviews to reports. I did not know any other person who made a living by digging into the most intimate facets of the people he was hired to investigate. I thought Rad was very thorough at his job.

"Satana was a Mexican national in the U.S. illegally. She collapsed in a commercial laundry where she'd been working for about a month, at less than minimum wage, twelve hours a day. No one at the laundry acknowledged that they even knew her. The hospital wasn't sure about the name. But no one really cared. The baby was bureaucratically carted off. It was a stroke of luck for the kid that the Vargas family had a timely charitable urge. They eventually picked her out of the thousands of kids that were available for adoption in southern California."

"And Rachel knows all this?"

"Yes. Old man Vargas told her everything as soon as she was old enough to understand. It was his way of being honest with her, at least that's what he explained to me. But he also had to interpret why she didn't have the same, uh, priority I guess is the word, as her brothers and sister."

"Brothers and sister?"

"Right. Rachel was stuck in the middle of three other kids. One older brother, and two younger siblings. Old man Vargas was willing to do his good deed for the little orphan, but he also made it clear that his real children got all that they deserved, and more."

He balanced his computer on his knees so that he could frame the word *real* with his fingers as quotation marks.

"Rachel was always the odd man out, so to speak. Don't get me wrong. Rachel was loved and taken care of, quite well. I have no doubt that Oscar Vargas loves Rachel and is worried about her. It's just never been quite the same between the father and the adopted daughter as between him and the other children. The quirks of a rich man, I guess."

"Yeah, I guess. And how about between Rachel and her mother?"

"Mrs. Vargas died a few months after the last child was born, when Rachel was about nine. The baby's name was Patricia. Her older brother, Jaime, was twelve, and the younger one, Francisco, was five. Not good family planning, if you ask me."

"Where are the brothers and sisters now? Aren't they worried about their missing sister?"

"I've only talked with Jaime, the eldest. He seemed very concerned. Gave me pictures of Rachel, provided the address in Mexico, even dug up the names and addresses of some of her friends. If the implication in your question is that maybe there are jealous relations who might be behind Rachel's disappearance, I didn't get that from Jaime. But I only met with him a few times. I haven't talked with the others since they were kids. They've been off at school and other things that rich brats do when they're young and on the loose."

I had to stand up. My knee had begun to throb and that was always a signal that I had to move it around, make the blood pump and flow before it tightened and left me with a painful, sleepless night. The painkillers from the ambulance driver hadn't lasted nearly long enough. I talked as I dragged my leg around my desk. Rad had implied that his connection with Rachel was more than a simple missing-person gig. I danced around the nagging loose ends of his story.

"It just hit me. Her father, her adoptive father, was named Oscar. Does that have anything to do with her fantasy about Acosta?"

"Oscar Acosta is one part of this that I can't get any kind of handle on. About two years ago, she became obsessed with what she called the Chicano Movement, the Hispanic civil rights protests of the sixties and seventies. Farmworkers, student sit-ins, La Raza Unida, the Crusade for Justice. She read everything she could about those times and those people. It was as if she needed that history to give herself some history. And then when she came across this guy Oscar Acosta—that was it. She told me that reading his book triggered all kinds of memories that she had forgotten. She recalled a dream, at least she always thought it was a dream, about time she spent with a big bluster of a man when she was a very small child, an infant. She told me that she couldn't shake the impression that the two of them were on the run, hiding from something. She convinced herself that Acosta was her father, even though she didn't have any kind of evidence. And then, out of the blue, she dropped the news on me that she had been contacted by him and was arranging a meeting. That's when I got worried about her, about her health, you know, her mental state. I talked her into letting me go along to this meeting with Acosta or whoever he was. But she already had her trip to Mexico set, and the guy hadn't finalized anything by the time she left. From the way she described what was going on, he was doing all his talking with Rachel on the phone. Then she left for Mexico, and that was the last time I saw her."

"It's weird, for sure. Her infatuation with writing a book must have come from her idealization of Acosta. Like father, like daughter? She was working on something, a book, that she was ardent about. You know that, right?"

"Sure. She writes very entertaining articles. We've talked about that, we've gone over ideas for her writing."

"And why does she call herself Espinoza? Vargas must be a name that could work wonders for her, no matter what she decided to do with her life."

He nodded.

"Yes, you're right. But that's the way Rachel is. She

used different names, for her writing she told me. It was another of her idiosyncrasies. She seemed to like Espinoza. According to her, it came from the Spanish for thorn—*espina*—and she liked to think of herself like that. But thorn can in turn mean other things that she related to."

That all clicked, in a way I did not completely understand. She was adopted, not sure about her father. Why not try different names until you found one you liked? *Estar en espinas*—to be on edge, suspicious. Rachel the prickly thorn in somebody's side, or Rachel the suspicious one?

I asked another question.

"Why didn't you tell me from the beginning that you and she were friends? You knew her and her family, evidently for years. This is more than just a paycheck. Can you still be professional about finding her, Rad? I know what it means to get involved emotionally in a case or a client. In the long run, it doesn't work."

I was behind him so I couldn't see his face. Rad paused, sipped his drink, then put the glass down on my desk. He finally answered me, but his voice had changed. He did not sound as young. His tone held that same quickness and deadliness he had exhibited against the unlucky Torres brothers.

"I've known Rachel for a few years. We became very close. I planned to marry her. That's why I know I'll find her. No one can stop me, Montez. And if someone has harmed her in any way, I'll make them pay, one way or another. But I'll do my job right. Mr. Vargas hired me because I'm good, and because he knew nothing would stop me from finding Rachel. Anyone who doubts that and thinks they can play me because of my relationship with Rachel will be disappointed, very disappointed, and extremely sorry. You can count on that, Louie."

I did not doubt it.

"So now what? What else do you have to go on? What's your next step?"

He set his computer case on the floor near his feet.

"I have a reservation tomorrow on a flight for Missoula, Montana. I'm going to talk with Mel Kodiack, the writer who shared the condo with her. I've never met him. She never let me go along on those trips. Said she had to be immersed in writing to accomplish what she wanted to, so she spent time with other writers, or by herself. Kodiack was down there when she disappeared. I'm sure he has something to tell me. As soon as I finish with you."

"Me? I've told you everything, Rad. I hope you find her. I hope it turns out. I'm actually sorry you're leaving. I thought you could contribute to piecing together a version of the truth about the 'Hole fire for Bonnie Collins. But there isn't anything else I know about Rachel Espinoza that I can pass on to you. Nothing."

He turned in his chair and faced me. The light on the desk cast an aura of yellow haze around his head. I couldn't see his eyes but I felt their gaze.

"Louie, I know Rachel. I know that she couldn't resist talking about her ambitions about writing. She talked to everybody about that. She loved her book, she wanted everybody to read it. And so she passed out copies of it everywhere she went, including Mexico. I'd bet that after she met you, she brought up her novel, and she probably gave you a copy. And that copy is most likely the last thing she wrote on before she disappeared. She always made notes to herself about things going on around her, and those notes ended up in her boxes of manuscripts. So, Louie, where's the book?"

6

◆

I liked the kid. He seemed to have a good heart, a functioning brain, and a progressive attitude about fashion. That was plenty more than I had come to expect from most of the young *raza* I bumped into through my clients or the occasional social outings I managed. But love can work in strange ways, even on the best of men, and Rad's affection for Rachel had made him a bit testy—I might even say on edge.

I walked around my desk and faced him so that we both shared the light.

"I'm not clear myself about why I didn't show you her book, Rad. I guess I wanted to look it over when I had a chance. Maybe there was something I overlooked the first time I went through it. I didn't see anything unusual or suspicious when I first read her story, but I didn't know the context, you know what I mean? Looking at it now, with the stuff on Rachel that you gave me, might give me an idea, or something. Hell, I don't know. But you can look at it. I'm not trying to keep it from you."

"I hope not. I'd regret it if you were trying to send me down the wrong track. I want to trust you, Louie."

"Well, good. We understand each other. The book's in my file cabinet, back there in the corner. The middle drawer. Here's the key; it's locked."

I flipped him a small silver key that I had taken out of the top drawer of my desk. He caught it and turned to the file cabinet. From out of nowhere, he yanked on the drawer before he tried the key. He fell backward as the drawer slid out of its runners and crashed back against his leg. He caught himself against my desk. The file drawer was empty. Rad Valdez looked at me, dropped the drawer, and glared.

"You're fucking with me, man. I told you not to do that. Where's the goddamn book?"

He did not shout, did not raise his voice, not one decibel. He was under control, but there was no doubt that he was threatening me. I braced myself and prepared to meet him head-on.

"Check out the lock, Rad. Somebody must have jimmied it. Someone stole the damn thing, don't you see? The book was in there, locked up. The last time I saw it was about a week ago. I thought the only person who knew I had it was Rachel. But there's somebody else, and he took it."

Valdez stopped moving toward me. He went back to the file cabinet and tried to look at the lock and the runners for the drawer.

He muttered, "Damn!" then abruptly moved to the wall, where he hit the switch for the overhead light. White spots and streaks popped in my eyeballs.

Rad carefully inspected the cabinet and the drawer. I

moved closer and, after my eyes adjusted, could see for myself that the inside edges of the lock were bent and chipped. It was a cheap file cabinet and it wouldn't have taken much to pry it open. Rad replaced the drawer in the cabinet and closed it. With the drawer in place, there was no way to tell that the lock was broken.

"This doesn't mean crap. I don't know if you ever had the manuscript in here, or how long this thing's been broken, or anything else about your story. If you've got the book, give it up. You're only mucking up my job if you're trying to put one over on me."

"No way, Rad. I don't have to jerk you around. I met Rachel once. She gave me her book. I didn't do anything to her, I didn't have her kidnapped, I don't know anything about her father except what you've told me, and the only thing I ever knew about Oscar Acosta I learned from that paperback on my desk. Someone broke into my house and stole her papers. I'm the one who ought to be pissed. This is my office, my *house,* for Christ's sake! And it means that somebody knows a lot about Rachel, including who she gave her manuscripts to, and now I feel like I'm somebody's target, and I don't even know for what!"

He relaxed, and his enigmatic smile returned.

"I shouldn't, but I believe you. I think you're right. Obviously, there's someone who thought the book was important, and that has to be related to Rachel's disappearance. For me that means that Rachel is in more trouble than I thought. Someone is trying to cover his tracks. Rachel's manuscript has something that this person, whoever he is, doesn't want out in the open because whatever happened to Rachel wasn't voluntary. And because there hasn't been any ransom demand, that means that her disappearance had nothing to do with kidnapping, unless it was a snatch that went bad. It's more than kidnapping, much more."

I felt the edge of my chair against the back of my legs and I bent into my space behind my desk. Rad remained standing but his mind was a long way from that room. We stared at each other. A very real possibility had changed the picture. We had to be thinking the same thing, a thought that neither of us wanted to give life to by uttering. "Much more than kidnapping" meant only one other alternative—murder.

Bobby Baca could be mean. As far back as I could remember, he had always been an angry man—mad at a world he believed was unfair, downright bad, a world he tried to understand but often couldn't. Maybe it was a lack of patience.

He was younger than I, but we both had attended the university on the northern edge of the state where we launched our revolutions, private and political. He kept on with the movement after the bunch of rowdies I had hung out with on campus had moved on, including myself. But I had watched him from afar. He lashed out at what I thought were insignificant slights or inflated abuses, and because those were days of collective anger, he manipulated his outbursts in front of appreciative and uptight audiences who had their own legitimate grievances, but who, more often than not, adopted Bobby's agenda. He had that way. Bobby Baca was a man for whom I could never be Chicano enough—I could never be that proud, that angry, nor could I carry such a large chip on my shoulder.

His anger stoked his energy, and he first garnered a reputation as a speaker—a rapper—whose well-turned phrases could ignite a crowd, and when that act wore itself out, he turned to the written word. He tried to cope with the hated world with his poetry, and so he had become an angry poet. Eventually his reputation as a poet was built more on his delivery of his phrases than their effect from the silent page.

Baca wrote powerful, moving words that flew from his mouth and then tore at the listener's soul like hurled razors slashing a stretched, delicate ribbon. I loved his poetry; it made me stop and think, and sometimes choke up. I just didn't like *him* all that much.

A legendary temper fueled his bigger-than-life persona: student activist tossed out of college because of a tempestuous blowup with one of his professors during a debate about the need for Chicano studies; a popular politician ready with a colorful quote who never got elected to anything more important than one term on the city's school board but who always managed to get himself included in the Democratic Party forums, fundraisers, and media events; and, most recently, cultural poet, small-time publisher, and all-around community fix-it guy. And, in my eyes his most important trait, literary comrade of Charlotte Garcia.

He pulled back the door to his house and a surprised smile opened his face. He gathered me in his arms. I hugged him back, timidly. I never was good at hugging other men in public, even though it's supposed to be a sign of Chicano brotherhood.

I started to apologize for dropping by so late, but he interrupted me.

"Louie! Man, I was just thinking of you. *¡Qué* serendipitous! Come in, come in! Give me your advice, guy. I'm working on Charlotte's book and I need an introduction, something from the heart that only a good friend can say.

I thought, maybe, you know how it is, that you could write it. What you say, *hermano?*"

He had caught me off guard. I tried to express why I shouldn't do what he had asked, but I couldn't come up with anything honest.

"Well, uh, well—let me think about it, okay? You're the writer, not me. I don't know, I . . ."

I trailed off when I saw the pages of the book he had been working on, spread out on a small table in his cluttered living room. I sat on his couch and hurriedly picked up the pages of the book. Charlotte's sensual and precise poetry captured me instantly, as it always had, and I had to clear my throat of sentiment.

"This looks good. You and Chavez have a nice start here."

"Yeah, I think so. That old wino can still paint a pretty picture, no? His drawings will add just the right touch to what I'm trying to do for Charlotte. But I'm serious, Louie. I need an intro. And you can write, man! You're a fucking lawyer. Think about it and let me know. Seriously. Okay?"

"I will. I'll think it over. I've never done anything like that. What you're doing for her is good, Bobby, real good. I wouldn't want to screw it up. That's all it is. I wouldn't want to screw it up."

"You want something to drink? *¿Cerveza, vino?*"

"No, thanks. I don't want to take up too much of your time, and I'm kind of here on business. I dropped by because I wanted to ask you a few questions. About the fire, and what happened that night. It's for Bonnie. I promised her I would check it out as much as I could, and I was hoping that maybe you saw something that maybe you didn't mention before, something that came to you now that it's been a few days. You know what I mean?"

He slowly nodded his head.

"Sure, man, sure. But you have to know as much as I do. That fucking fire was so fast, I barely managed to get the hell out of there before the shack exploded. Me and Donna tore out of there like a couple of scared *conejos*. And poor Charlotte! I lost track of her when that bomb flew through the window. Too much smoke and fire and panic. They ought to take whoever did it and . . ."

He did not have to finish. Among her friends and in the community where she had lived, there was universal agreement that Charlotte's murderer deserved nothing better than a slow, painful execution. And plenty of people were willing to volunteer as executioner.

"Did you ever hear Charlotte say she was worried about anybody? Threats, arguments, anything like that? Do you recall anyone she ever had a disagreement with? I can't imagine it myself, but if there was anything . . . ?"

He sat on a straight-backed, rather flimsy-looking chair that tried hard to copy the style of the Spanish colonialists. He rubbed his chin and stared past me.

From where I sat I could see his front yard through a large bay window. The night was parted by the bright, glaring beam of a streetlight near his multicolored picket fence. In the light and framed by the night, the fence looked gray.

"I hate doing this, man. I've thought about her so much since she died. The only thing that's popped in my mind is that incident with Michaelson, that assistant principal from North High who didn't want her talking to any of the students in the Hispanic literature course. Too radical for him, I guess, not Christian enough, he said one time. There was a brouhaha with some of the students, a couple of meetings, and then it died down. One day she read her poetry to the students, no one dropped out or became a devil worshiper, and Michaelson moved on to one of those private charter schools. But that was last winter, and it wasn't the kind of thing that could lead to something like the fire. It couldn't have been him, could it?"

"I doubt it. I remember a little bit about that. Bruce Michaelson was a creep, but not an arsonist. I guess it wouldn't hurt to check it out, though. Anything else?"

He gave me a look that said he was getting impatient with my questions. It was late, and he still had work to do, so I stood as a sign that I was willing to end the discussion.

He quickly moved from the chair and opened his door for me.

"There's nothing else I can think of. Charlotte just didn't have enemies. You know that. My gut is that it was those fucking punks, probably that kid Sanchez. They were high, thought it would be cool to watch the fire, and maybe a few people run in terror, and they end up killing Charlotte. I hope they go down, all those punk bastards!"

We said our good-byes and I left. He had provided one piece of information that I had forgotten—Michaelson. And he had confirmed the general assumption held by most of Charlotte's friends: The kids had set the fire and Charlotte Garcia was their unintentional victim. I had no grounds to suspect otherwise.

Baca lived a half-dozen blocks from the 'Hole. During the drive to my house, I listened to a late-night talk show. I wasn't in the mood for music, so I turned on the background noise of a host and his caller as they dissected the murder trial of the century going on back in decadent, deadly Los Angeles. Celebrity defendants and big-money defense lawyers had no place in the community I drove

58

through in darkness. This was a place of the working poor, of pride and determination, but also a place of disaffected youth, frustrated teachers, exhausted parents, and jaded cops who had already solved the murder of Charlotte Garcia, at least in their own minds. This was a place where murder could be accomplished with a bottle of cheap gas and an oily rag. The case against Charlotte's killer would have no DNA evidence, no high-profile experts from around the world, no televisions in the courtroom.

I drove past the Keyhole, still cordoned off with police warnings and tape. Nothing remained of the building except a pile of charred roof beams and a forlorn cluster of wounded bricks.

I told myself that I had to move away from complicating Charlotte's murder. Maybe the kids, the punks as Baca had called them, were the killers.

But, for a few minutes, I silently questioned why Bobby Baca hadn't mentioned that he had also argued with Charlotte, and not only in the friendly debate I had witnessed at the 'Hole the night of the fire. Of course, they had patched things up, and they were close friends, I did not doubt that. They did readings together, and assisted each other with their respective projects. Charlotte wrote for Baca's magazine, when it came out, and Bobby had found a publisher for one of her collections. So there was no need for him to mention himself when I asked about any arguments Charlotte might have had.

You're no investigator, Montez, I thought. Too paranoid. Maybe it's your nature now, considering everything you've been through lately. But still . . .

I saved it for my breakfast meeting with Rad, when we planned to review what each of us had found out from our respective assignments that last night the detective planned to be in Denver.

7

—◆—

"A hearty western breakfast, just what the doctor ordered."

With that introduction, Rad stormed into over-easy eggs, a slab of ham, crispy hash browns, buttery toast, dollar-sized pancakes, orange juice, and milked-down coffee as though he were getting ready to board the bus to the state pen rather than a jet to Montana. I picked at what the waitress had assured me was a delicious breakfast burrito. The stiff tortilla wrapped around red chili beans and a watery green sauce bore no resemblance to anything my mother or father had ever served me for breakfast. Somewhere on my plate lay a well-hidden scrambled egg.

"I wonder why none of these breakfast joints serves fried baloney, *refritos,* and chopped-up eggs smothered in catsup? Now *that* was the breakfast of champions in my house."

Rad's look of disgust passed quickly. He brought up

one of our favorite topics of conversation.

"Of his two books, I think I prefer *Revolt of the Cockroach People.* At least I learned some history from that one. I borrowed copies from Rachel right after she started telling me about her supposed old man. But I got to say, Louie, that guy was wild, a *loco,* like you would put it. You ask me, his writing was weak, but he told a good story, even if I thought it was fifty percent BS and fifty percent acid trip. If any of that stuff is true, then, in addition to everything else, he was a druggie, womanizer, emotionally unstable, and a terrorist on top of all that."

"So?"

He shook his head at my apparent obtuseness.

"So, I researched the guy. Read things about him. Magazine articles, a couple of essays. Thompson's pieces. One day there will be a serious book about him. But honestly, I don't get what you and Charlotte saw in that guy—the way you make him out to be a legend. I wouldn't exactly call him a role model."

Man, oh man. Trying to explain Zeta was a waste of time, and to boot, Rad had read the books! He talked on about what he thought he knew about Buffalo Z. Brown, in between mouthfuls of breakfast.

"The way he supposedly died, for example. The story about taking off in that boat in 'seventy-four and then disappearing fits in with his larger-than-life romantic image, but not everyone he knew buys it. Another version has it that he was a drug trafficker and one of his deals blew up. There was an argument, a shooting, and that's the end of Acosta. Now that version has a ring of truth to it, and many of his acquaintances accept it."

I reined in my frustration, and thought I could make my point by sneaking up on it.

"Check this out, Rad. Maybe it's not important about

the way he died, but the way he lived, and what he did when he was alive. He made a difference. You might not see it because today, all around us, we are surrounded by the rip-off of our culture. We take many things for granted."

He nodded.

"Sure, that's true. Hispanics are in. That's another problem I have with some of what you and Charlotte and the others in the Keyhole were talking about. What's the beef? What's the deal today, man? Not twenty or thirty years ago when things were different, I'll give you that. But today—it's a brand-new bag."

"New bag, same old junk inside. Sure, your history and background, even if you don't know it that well, are plastered everywhere—making money for someone else. In the face of English-only crap, and anti-immigrant hysteria, and the ever-expanding divisions between races and nationalities. Still, with all that going on, you are right, to a point. Hispanics, as you say, are what's happening. Cinco de Mayo celebrations—sponsored by politicos and the chamber of commerce. Fast-food taco joints and Mexican beer commercials. Some movies based on our stories, but seldom with our actors. Mexican-American mayors, with their own scandals."

His smile was infectious, and I had to grin. He said, "Kind of like a Chicano renaissance? Sounds cool to me."

"Sure, you could say that. And, it's cool with me, too. Documentaries and books about the movement are coming out left and right. Even the old-timers are getting something out of it. Bobby Baca has a deal in the works to republish his old stuff. I hear it will be quite a production."

"There you go, Louie."

I turned off the grin and tried to sound serious.

"But even though we may be the 'in' ethnic group this year, our poverty rate continues to climb, the dropout numbers go up, our men in penitentiaries do harder time, and we are still losing ground on every important economic scale. There's a huge backlash about affirmative action programs, but what's that about? Are those programs actually working, which means that people who look like you and me and Rachel might land someplace important one day? We may be everywhere, Rad, but, like most things in life, that's good and bad."

He waited for more but it wasn't coming.

"And what? That's it? Cinco de Mayo is an annual beer-drinking party and I should be grateful to Oscar Acosta for that? Sorry, man, I can't get behind that."

"All I can say is that during those times in his books, back when I was a young guy like you, Chicanos were around, obviously, we were living in this state, but there wasn't anything about us, anywhere. In some places it was illegal to speak Spanish in public. That's in Zeta's books. Chicano kids in school didn't have much of a chance, unless they had incredible luck, or balls, like Acosta. A federal judge in this state laughed out loud, in his courtroom, at the people from the San Luis Valley who tried to use the system to protect their rights to their land. A trite term back then was that we were the sleeping giant, waiting to wake up and kick the society that had ignored us and put us down. But I always thought that image was wrong. We weren't sleeping, and we certainly were no giant. We were individuals and families busting our asses, running scared, doing the best we could. We were called pachucos, zoot suiters, braceros, wetbacks, Spanish-surnamed, greasers and spics, dirty Mexicans—everything except what we really are because we didn't have a face, a consciousness—no identity, man. Not until we understood about being Chicano. And that's where Zeta comes in. He understood. About identity, about struggle. He wasn't perfect. I never said he was, nor would anyone else who knows anything about the guy. He had a serious problem relating to women at the same level, at least that's what comes out in his books. But he did what he had to do, as crazy as necessary, because that was the only way! Nothing else would have worked back then."

I thought I had him. He watched me, fascinated maybe, and he quit eating. I kept on.

"But it was only a stage, Rad. An absolutely essential, required, historically manifested piece of our people's progress, but it was only a stage. One day we will move past the Cinco de Mayo period into something else, and there will be more and crazier Zetas. That's the way it is, Rad. Maybe you should read his books again."

He might not argue with me, but, deep down, I argued with myself. As I talked, I did not swallow everything I mouthed. I couldn't. Why did I have to drag out the old Chicano rap? Why did I insist on lionizing dead heroes and villains? I hadn't thought about Acosta in years. Where had this nonsense about stages and people's progress come from? ¡Ay, Louie! *Cuídate*, bud.

Rad sucked in a deep breath and picked up his fork again.

"I like your slant on identity. Although even you got to admit that we just keep going through the same old arguments. Before it was Chicano or Mexican-American. Now it's Hispanic or Latino. And don't you dare forget Hispana/Latina. I get confused, man. For you, Louie, what I will do is keep an open mind about the man. But I can't read his books. I couldn't do it again. I'll pick up something else about him."

65

"If you can find it."

"Yeah, sure."

I did not tell him that I admired Zeta for other considerations, not the least of which had to do with the connection I felt between my own coming-of-age experience and the Buffalo's lifestyle. Drug and alcohol binges, endless frenetic parties, hanging out with the wildest Anglo kids, pushing the limits of excess—I could relate to all of that. Zeta wrote about my youth, and I inwardly thanked him for doing that favor for me and all the other *locos* who grew up during the revolution. While watching young Rad with his ubiquitous smile and his calculated doubt, my appreciation of Oscar Acosta did not seem to have much to do with politics.

For several minutes we concentrated on our breakfast. He ate chunks of early-morning cholesterol and I drank heavy doses of caffeine. Finally, he turned to the real business at hand.

"Your conversation with Baca has some potential, but I wouldn't get too wrapped up in it. From what you've told me, Michaelson's not the torch, and Bobby had nothing to do with the fire. He was in the place, remember? He'd have to be either very stupid or very smart to try to burn down a place while he was in it. He doesn't strike me as either. And he has no motive. That argument you described doesn't amount to much. That's what's screwy about the whole deal. No one that I know about had a motive to kill Charlotte, or to even get rid of the 'Hole. Nothing shady about Donna or her old man, Cal. And I'm satisfied that the fire couldn't have been aimed at Charlotte. Too hit-or-miss. I suppose it could have been meant for someone else in the place, but, jeez Louise, what a long shot. It was a very inefficient way to try to kill someone, if you ask me."

"Your visit with Donna and Cool Cal didn't turn anything up, then?"

He had to wait to respond until he finished chewing on his pancakes and eggs. I sipped more coffee.

"They're intriguing people, I'll say that. You didn't mention that this guy Calvin Maestas is a midget. But other than that wrinkle, I didn't learn anything of note. They couldn't fill in any holes. I'm afraid, Louie, that your friend Bonnie will have to go on without knowing anything more about the death of Charlotte, at least for now. One day the cops will snag somebody for this. It was too careless, too spontaneous, and those kinds of crimes usually open up of their own accord. Loose lips in a bar, or a deal in some other bust. Know what I mean?"

I nodded, and drank my coffee and ignored the mess on my greasy plate. Cool Cal was short, but a midget?

The coffee had impressed me and that made me think of Jesús, my aged father who spent most of his time piddling around his house with a coffee cup in his hand, telling me his memories, sometimes repeatedly. He once told me about a shooting, a fight, and the supposed spontaneous nature of the violence that eventually influenced a jury to let the shooter go. The trial and its aftermath were history, except that my father knew the truth and it wasn't exactly what the jury had believed. That had happened so many years ago that I knew there was no record of the case, and so I couldn't prove my father right or wrong. But I believed him. Hey, he's my old man.

I wrote a note to myself on a napkin. *Talk to J about shooting. Details?* The remembrance had come to me like a cold shot, a non sequitur. I would follow up on it because it was easy and it had some relevance—obscure, to be sure, but at least I had these pieces of history. I stuffed the napkin in my pocket, handed the check to the detective with the expense account, and eventually ushered Rad to my car and then to the airport.

I waited with him inside the terminal of Stapleton International. I told him jokes about the much-delayed opening of Denver International and he laughed politely. One day, he assured me, Denver would have an airport we would brag about.

He talked about Rachel and his search. He intended to find all the people who had shared the Mexican condo, then follow any leads that developed from his interviews. Mel Kodiack represented the first step in that process. I brought up the untidy problem of the stolen manuscript. I did not want him to remind me about it, but we both agreed that I had to watch my step and let him know if I thought of anything or uncovered something he could use. He scribbled his pager number on another one of his cards.

Finally, he assured me that I would see him again. We parted on good terms, shaking hands and exchanging halfhearted *abrazos*, but we both knew that his incentive was tied around the thin but burning memory of Rachel, and good terms were not enough to keep Rad off my back when it came to his fantasy. Love and war—friends don't mean a thing in either one.

8

⬥

Jesús Genaro Montez needed a shave. The gray-and-white growth of three days of beard had a silk-like, almost angel's-hair texture, but it had to go. I lathered his face and then I glided his Trac II across his wrinkled skin—slowly, oh so slowly. The razor had a chipped handle with a veneer of old soap, but with a fresh cartridge it worked fine.

"Be careful, Louie. I ain't got much blood left, and I don't want to lose any because of your shaky hands. You drink too much, son."

"My hands don't shake, but your face sure quivers and quakes. Be still, or we will have a bloodletting. Pretend you're in the barbershop. Gee, Dad, you should try to keep on top of this personal grooming stuff."

"I'm almost eighty years old. Everyone I ever knew is either dead, in the hospital, or in a nursing home. Who am I trying to impress? Shaving is the biggest crime ever inflicted on men. I hate it, always have. This is to shut you up. Otherwise I wouldn't bother. And I haven't been to a barber since Emiliano croaked that day we were all in his shop."

"That was at least ten years ago. Who cuts your hair?"

"That's for me to know, and you to mind your own business."

"I don't know, Jesús. You worry me some days."

He started to laugh but he ended up coughing. I waited while he brought his heaving body back under control. I turned down his radio and opened the kitchen window to relieve some of the trapped heat that Jesús had allowed to accumulate in his house. A mix of traffic and hollering children competed with a Mexican music station deejay who jabbered about an upcoming concert at the Adams County Fairgrounds. Ostensibly, the greatest recording artists in the history of Mexico planned to grace the stage the next Saturday night, and tickets were only twenty-five bucks for a couple.

Five minutes later, I finished with his face and rinsed the razor, the soap brush, and the lather cup. He did not use prepackaged shaving cream.

Jesús said he might go to the dance.

I did not react to that statement. I calculated that in the past ten years he had been to a barber more often than he had dragged himself to a dance hall.

"I wanted to talk with you about something that happened back in the thirties. A story of yours that I remember hearing only once, when I was a kid. I think Mom made you tell it, I can't even remember why. You know what I mean, that one about the shooting, in Chandler. You were arrested, your trial and all that. There's something about all that's happened lately that reminded me of that story, but I think I'm just more curious than anything else."

He poured two cups of coffee, handed me one, and made himself comfortable in his big easy chair. He patted his face.

"That stuff you put on my skin smells kind of like anise. What is it? Stings, too."

"Aftershave. Old Spice. You had a bottle in your medicine chest. Whatever it is, it's yours."

"*¡Santo Niño,* Louie! That stuff is as old as you. No wonder it's burning a hole in my cheek. It must be pure alcohol. What a guy!"

He made a show of wiping his face with his handkerchief.

"I think you'll live, Dad."

"Yeah, sure. With a burned-off jaw."

He sputtered for a few more minutes, then returned to my question.

"Anyway, that story. It had nothing to do with a fire, for starters. I don't like it because I'm not proud of what happened. Those were different times, different people."

"It's part of my history, too, Dad. I should know it."

"Yes, you may be right."

A slight pause, then his words drowned out the radio noise and the exterior hum.

"I was a young man, maybe twenty. We lived for a time in Chandler, down by Florence. Chandler's gone now, and the only clues that it ever existed are the crumbling pieces of building foundations. They moved all the houses when the mine finally played out. But when I lived there, it was a lively mining town and the miners were all *Mexicanos* or *Italianos.* The mine was owned by a man from Cañon City. I worked the mine, and so did most of my family—the uncles and cousins I lived with in those years. I was the shift foreman. Even if I have to say it, I worked hard. I was honest and kept the men at it, so the company liked me, respected me even though I was a *Mexicano*. The men respected me, too. Most of them, anyway."

For a few seconds, he stared through me while his brain put the pieces of his past in place, and his mouth found the words that brought back the events.

"For someone like that, there's always somebody else who resents him, who challenges him, even though it may be all one-sided. There was a guy, Alejandro Ozuna. I think he thought he was in a feud with our family. None of us did."

"But he never really took you on, right? It was always someone else in the family, no?"

"Yes, that's right. He left me alone, I think, because of my position in the mine. But my brother-in-law, Samuel, was a different story. Samuel was young, younger than me, but much taller than Ozuna. He was hell. Quick to respond to provocation. A quick temper. He and Ozuna did not mix well."

I moved the story along with some of the details that I remembered from the one time I had heard this particular chapter of his life and the few times he had told his children other tales of his youth.

"It came to a head at one of the house parties the miners had every Friday night. I remember you talking about them. Every week a different house, but always the same party. Liquor, music, dancing, card games. Until the sun came up. And the men checked their guns at the front table. Rows of guns laid out that weren't touched until the party was over."

"Yes, that's how it was. I can still see the barrels of those guns. Long and shiny, resting next to each other like pipes on an organ."

"And at one of the parties, this guy Ozuna decided to resolve his feud, for a purpose only he knew."

"It sounds trite now, but it's true. Our lives were hard and the times were mean. *Yo era muy joven,* but I remember that part of my life as if it was only yesterday. We knew only work. Death came suddenly and often. Accidents in the mines, illness, and our anger. We had nothing except our friends and families. We had no country. Most of the men could not return to Mexico; everyone was escaping from something. And those of us who traced roots for more than a hundred years in this land, back before it suddenly turned into the United States, we also had no place. It had been taken from us. Men were quick to react because a delay could cost a life. Ozuna knew that, and that was how he acted that night."

He lapsed into Spanish.

Jesús cinched the holster around his waist and checked the chamber of his revolver. He belched, then slipped the weapon into its resting place. Samuel had disappeared, but Jesús could not wait. The sun soon would rise above the background silhouette of the Sangre de Cristo Mountains, and he needed sleep. Only one day off from the mines, and it should be a day of rest. Most of his money changed hands during the card game, and he had not found the opportunity to dance with Marie. The night had not been a good one. Ozuna had taunted the other card players for the entire game. The whiskey mellowed some of the edginess, but Jesús had not had enough of that. He was not drunk.

Manuel handed him his hat and wished him a safe journey back to the house where he lived with several members of his brother's wife's family.

"Next week, the game will be at your house," Manuel reminded him. Jesús stepped into the night.

He normally walked straight down the road from

Manuel's home. Chandler was a small town with only a few streets. Even so, the Mexicano workers lived near each other and the Italians shared the other half of the town.

The cold minutes before dawn hit him as soon as he left the warmth of Manuel's house. He buttoned his thin coat and pulled down his hat's wide brim in a futile gesture to protect the back of his neck. The night air, the cold air, magnified sounds, and his ears picked up the howling Sarmiento dog, and the icy bubbling creek at the edge of the town. An angry man's words raced across that same air, and stopped him.

"You've laughed at me for the last time. Prepare for God or the devil!"

He jumped, frightened, but the words were not meant for him. Jesús rushed to the back of Manuel's house, quietly, and with an urgency that made his temples throb. He stood at the corner of the house, in the darkness, and watched Samuel and Alejandro. The two men faced each other across the bare yard. Ozuna's gun stuck out from the top of his trousers, near his right hand. Samuel had no weapon. He had stepped outside for air without retrieving his gun from the front table.

"¡Cabrón! You are not man enough!"

Samuel, the boy, was drunk and he twisted in the blackness as he spoke. He spit at Ozuna, then turned his back. Jesús flinched. His brother-in-law had made a mistake. Ozuna reached for his gun and pointed it at Samuel's back. Jesús gripped the leathery handle of his revolver, eased it from his holster, aimed, and fired. The roar echoed in the night and rang in his ears. An orange flame flowered at the end of his gun for an instant. His hand kicked back from the gun's reflex. Ozuna spun in the dirt, reached for his side, dropped his gun, and fell. Samuel collapsed to his knees, then tried to make sense out of the night and the wounded man sprawled near him. Ozuna's spasms were quick and violent. A pool of black blood flowed into the frozen earth.

Manuel ran to the men with his own gun in his hand. The sun popped into view at the edge of the mountains, and Manuel could see that Ozuna was dead.

"I'll find the boss. He'll know what we should do."

He ran back to his house and told his wife to make some coffee. "We have a long morning ahead of us."

Jesús poured himself another cup of coffee as he neared the end of his story.

"The boss, the mine owner, *me conoció y me dió respeto,* but even he couldn't stop them from arresting me. I spent several weeks in the county jail in Cañon City. My family visited every week, but it was hard on them. When *el patrón* testified at my trial, that was all that the jury had to hear. I was the first *Mexicano* in Fremont County who wasn't convicted of the crime he had been charged with. The jury was made up of ranchers and other mine owners and a couple of shopkeepers. They appreciated that the boss thought well of me, that he came to the trial and testified that I was a good man, and that in his opinion, whatever I did was necessary. They let me go, calling the killing justified, and I went back to the mine, where I worked until the boss sold the mine to a company from the East. Samuel moved away, and we lost track of him. Ozuna's family kept up the feud with the Montez family for years. They made threats to avenge Alejandro's death, but nothing came of it. And now I have outlived them all."

I asked Jesús my questions.

"It sounds so quick and ugly, yet you reacted in the

blink of an eye, quite bravely. But there had to have been a risk to Samuel. In the darkness, with the two men so close to each other, and you slowed by liquor. Why didn't you holler, try to warn Samuel? For our family, it turned out right, but it could easily have gone the other way. What were you thinking when you shot Ozuna?"

My father pursed his lips, rubbed his forehead, and moved his tongue inside his cheek. His face carried the serious look that, of late, he had taken to wearing more often.

"As I said, Louie, men had to act quickly. That's the way those times were. I never liked to talk about the shooting, or the trial, or any of that. The Ozuna family left me alone. It was the rest of the Montez clan who had to fight with the Ozunas and put up with their insults. Since you ask, I had to shoot. A warning would only have delayed the inevitable. I always understood that I would have to do something very much like what went down that night. We all could see it coming, and so my actions that night were not as impulsive as my boss made them sound in the courtroom. Ozuna and a Montez had to have a resolution of whatever it was that worked on Ozuna's mind. He had to be stopped and that night, in that place, there was only one way—with the gun. If I missed and shot Samuel, well, maybe that would have been enough for Ozuna. Alejandro and Samuel were the same; they were both guilty of something that night, and all I could do was stop it. That's what I did."

"Cold-blooded, Dad. But I can see what you mean. At least I think I get it. Sometimes you lose me."

"Ha! The loser gets lost. *Pobrecito,* all that education and you can't understand the simple stories of your rickety old father. Louie, Louie. What am I going to do with you?"

9

◆

Jesús shook his head at me as I left with the excuse that I had to get back to work. But it wasn't an excuse, really. With Rad not taking up my time, and nothing new breaking on the Keyhole fire, I had a chance to work on the still immature sprouts of my rejuvenated practice. First on my list were Wilson Lopez and the disagreeable Albert Kopinski.

I'd filed my motions and we were set for a hearing. I hoped to convince Judge Lowell that Kopinski had flouted his orders—if not the precise letter of those orders, then certainly their spirit. However one looked at it, Kopinski had continued to try to squeeze money out of Lopez, and that was a no-no under the bankruptcy code.

That's when I had one of my famous bursts of creativity. On the way to my house/office, I pulled into the supermarket near my father's house and waited for a phone to call Lopez. The middle-aged cashier using the phone, either on an extended break or at the end of her shift, kept looking at me as I cleared my throat and generally made a subtle nuisance of myself. She took ten minutes to give the okay to her daughter for an overnight stay at Sharon's, whose description fluctuated between "that girl" and "that slut."

I thought, I've got to get a cell phone. Right. Immediately following a purchase of a new car, deposit on a new office, and the negotiated return of Aztlán to the reborn Chicano nation. And all that would happen as soon as my Lotto numbers clicked. Luis Montez, eternal optimist.

When I got my hands on the phone, I dialed Lopez. It took several minutes of begging, promises, and threats, but he reluctantly agreed to meet with Kopinski and me, if I could arrange it, for one last shot at a settlement.

"I'll try to get him to come by this evening. Maybe with the hearing hanging over his head he will be more agreeable than the last time we talked. I'll call and let you know. And leave the talking to me, understand?"

He said he did, but I knew he did not. I hung up the phone, then I called Kopinski. Before he could slam the phone in my ear, I blurted out that I needed to see him at six at my office, and that if he did not show up I would add more to what I would tell the judge about his contempt. I pleaded that it was his last chance to work things out.

He grumbled, "I'll be there, Montez. But I won't like it. This better be worth my time." *Then* he slammed the phone in my ear.

Feeling pretty good about myself, I handed the grimy receiver to a short, squat woman who had used a long shawl with an intricate weave to tie a bawling child to her waist. She jammed coins into the machine and almost immediately began shouting into the mouthpiece in fast, vulgar Spanish.

A ripple of doubt shimmied down my back, but I ignored it because I reasoned to myself that my uneasiness came from the bad vibes surrounding the public telephone and not anything to do with the reality of *In Re: Lopez*. Work things out, settle, mediate, arbitrate—these were the latest buzzwords of the legal profession. At least that's what the glossy insert in last Sunday's newspaper, written by a bar association PR person, had trumpeted to the public. I was only trying to do my part.

I parked my car in front of my house and sat behind the steering wheel for several minutes—thinking it through, forcing the brain to play lawyer. I envisioned myself persuading Kopinski that continuing to act like a *pendejo* would get him nowhere except on the wrong side of Judge Lowell. He would gradually understand the wisdom in my words, apologize to my client, and promise never to bother Lopez again. Everyone would shake hands, and my client and Kopinski would promise to get together and maybe even have a drink, for the old days. Lopez would be so grateful that he would pay his bill on the spot, in cash, just like the *Mexicanos* I represented in immigration hearings, and I would almost as quickly send off a check for my house payment, or office rent, however one wanted to look at it. My vision was practically enough to restore my faith in the legal profession.

Lopez arrived first and I talked to him about what I expected. He was my reluctant client, and any lawyer worth his Yellow Pages ad knows that he treads on slippery ground when his client feels bullied into going along.

"We don't lose anything, Wilson. If he doesn't want to work out an arrangement, then we do our thing at the contempt hearing. I'm trying to save you money. Look at it that way. My rate goes up for courtroom work, you know that."

He grunted, shook his head. We waited for Kopinski.

The windows rattled and my framed bar license shook against the wall. Thumps and booms from someone's outrageous car speakers rolled through the neighborhood.

Lopez twisted his hands together and sighed. "Damn kids. Northside's gone to hell. I'm getting out as soon as I fix this shit."

"You been here for about fifteen years, right? That how long you've known Kopinski?"

"Yeah, fifteen years, at least. I grew up in Brighton, back when it was out in the country."

Back when you were called Weeds, I thought, and it came to me that his boyhood moniker might have had more to do with his scrawny, blowing-in-the-wind frame than any all-night, freaky adventure in the tullies.

Lopez continued, "My family moved around, after the old man died, and I ended up in Denver, where I met Kopinski. He did some work on one of my trucks, back when I had my store, the carpet place. He was a different guy. But he's always in debt, always one step ahead of getting shut down for taxes or late loans. Money has always been a touchy subject with that guy."

Hello! Look who's talking, I wanted to say. Hey, Lopez, you're the guy who filed bankruptcy!

"What's the story on this ten grand, Wilson? How did you come to borrow money from this guy? What happened?"

"It wasn't a loan, at first. He needed me, at the beginning. I had sent him business from people I knew, talked him up at the Northside Optimists, got him some work from some businessmen I knew, and then one of my associates in El Paso. An import racket, but the trucks came through once a month, and every month, Kopinski could count on at least that one truck, for an oil change, lube, whatever. It wasn't much, I'm not saying that, but it was something. That's when we were friends. Like I told you, he came to my daughter's wedding, we spent time together. We took our wives to Vegas for a couple of years in a row. So he wanted to reciprocate when I got wiped out, when I had to close up my place. He said it was a present, but I told him no. What a stupid fuck I was back then! Live and learn, never too old. What a mess!"

"When I met with Kopinski, he made threats, against you and me. Said that if you didn't pay, you'd be visited by your mutual friend. What's that about?"

He scowled, and quit breathing. I waited, and, finally, he expelled air and released his tension.

"Damn! Kopinski, that, that . . . What can I say? Kopinski knows some rough people. There's a level he operates at, when he has to. You can see from the way he's reacted to my bankruptcy. He doesn't care about the way things are supposed to be done; he does them his own way. Always has. A few years back, when it was really tough for us, he introduced me to some of those people, and I was so on the edge that I let myself get talked into a deal with one of them. A guy who lends money, you know what I mean. But this guy wasn't just a loan shark. Nothing like that. He made me sign over a piece of the restaurant, as collateral, for a couple of thousand that I needed to keep it open. When I couldn't pay it back, the guy started to lean on me. Really lean on me. Kopinski bailed me out. Came up with the ten thousand that included the original loan and the additional bite. It adds up fast. Too fast for me, I found out. Kopinski came through, even though I didn't want it. I guess he saved my ass. All I can think of now is that this so-called mutual friend must be the same guy, or someone like him, who will enforce the debt. Too much, no?"

He looked at me with half-lidded eyes and his voice had dropped to a whisper. He acted guilty, and I did not sympathize. I was on Kopinski's side now that I knew the story. Hostile, angry Albert Kopinski had every right to expect that mousy, nervous Wilson Lopez would pay back the money that had protected Lopez's hide. What did a bankruptcy petition matter in this kind of situation?

"What's the name of this guy?"

"I knew him as Chick, and Albert called him Montero. He could have been Mexican or Italian. I tried not to get too close, or too nosy. He and his pals scared the hell out of me, and I learned from that experience, in more ways than one. That's when I first got a different feel for Albert Kopinski. Guess I was right."

Funny how some men think they learn from their experiences, but all they ever do is fool themselves.

We waited for more than an hour but Kopinski never showed up. My client's stake seemed less important to me after all I had learned, but there was no denying the fact that he was my client. I would see it through, at least as far as the contempt hearing, and then I would get out.

I telephoned Kopinski, but nobody answered. I finally accepted the obvious and told Wilson Lopez to go home.

"I guess we deal with this in the courthouse. I'll see you there, nine sharp. Okay?"

"Whatever you say, Montez. I hope this works."

He walked out of the house. I poured what was left of the Canadian whiskey into a glass and headed for the kitchen for some ice. My heart wasn't in *In Re: Lopez*. All it meant to me was a paycheck.

My fickle heart dropped into my guts and my drink crashed on the floor when I heard a loud thump and a ferocious whoosh from outside. It had to have been my car, hit by one of the slow-riding, boom-box-playing boys who couldn't see over the steering wheel. I stepped on broken glass, ran to the front of the house, and tried to see what had happened. I looked out the window into the early summer night until my eyes adjusted and I saw my car. I didn't waste too much time looking at it; it was all right. Wilson Lopez was sprawled across the pavement in front of my car and I could see that he wasn't all right. He was a long way from all right.

10

Kopinski has an alibi, of course?"

Two days after Weeds's death, Rad had returned a message I had left for him at his hotel in Missoula.

"A good one, too. Something he'd apparently forgotten about when I set up the meeting. Assisting the priest from Our Lady of Guadalupe. One of those trade-in-your-guns-for-a-holy-water-blessing events. Kopinski collected the guns, all eight of them. Surrounded by nuns, cops, and TV cameras. I've got to hand it to him, though. He hung up in my face when I finally reached him. First he told me that Lopez should rot in everlasting hell, and then that I would join him if I kept bugging him."

"Then he hung up?"

"Then he hung up. It's a bad habit he has."

"From here, Louie, I'd have to say that Kopinski and this guy Montero took care of business the old-fashioned way. You better watch yourself. Leave it. It's not really your concern anymore. And don't forget, somebody's on you about Rachel and her book. Almost sounds as though it's time for another vacation."

"*In Re: Lopez* may be, uh, in suspense, as they say down at the courthouse. And Weeds Lopez wasn't my idea of a good neighbor. But he was my client, Rad. There are a couple of loose strings that I need to tie up. He paid me to be his counselor and adviser. I guess I got to finish it. What's new with Rachel?"

I heard him sigh, and then a sound that must have been him sipping on a drink of some kind. Finally, he responded. "Too many dead ends. Mel Kodiack does his writing in a cabin along the Bitterroot River, and it was a bitch finding him. Claimed to be in the middle of his next book, and he didn't appreciate my intrusion. Very distrustful. Wouldn't tell me much until I showed him Rachel's photo and a letter from Oscar Vargas that introduced me and explained that I needed information about Rachel. That seemed to impress him. But he didn't give up much. He left Mexico on the same day that Rachel disappeared, but he thought she had just flown back to the States earlier in the day. He was upset about her vanishing act, but who knows for sure."

"Now what? The others who shared the condo?"

"There's only two. Brian Gulf, a screenwriter. Kodiack had his number and I'm meeting with him tomorrow back in L.A. Then a woman. One of Rachel's friends from UCLA. A performance artist, something like that. Her name's Isela Vega, but I haven't tracked her down yet. Kodiack claimed he didn't know her. Said Vega was long gone by the time he made it to Los Cabos. I feel uneasy about that guy."

"In what way? I thought he and Rachel were good friends."

A second of silence, then, "Yeah, friends."

He did not say anything more, and I did not have to be first in my class to understand that Rachel and Kodiack were lovers, and Rad either only suspected it, or he knew all about it and he didn't like it. I guess he didn't like it no matter what.

"Keep in touch, Rad. I may need your feet again. Kung fu and all that."

"Hah-hah. Yeah, you bet. Watch yourself."

During the call, Rad had told me that he had mailed a package of information that he thought I should have. He had copied some of his research, compiled a few notes, and put together a summary of where he was in his search for Rachel.

"There's something about the fire, and Charlotte, too, that you might find interesting. We can talk about it after you get a chance to look it over."

That was another point in Rad's favor. He gave the impression of saying only the most obvious things, but of knowing so much more that he wasn't telling, at least not when the listener wanted to hear it. It was part of his investigator's arsenal, like his martial arts expertise and the laptop computer. Maybe it was his way of finding out what he needed to know—he let others do the talking. How people responded to his silence or his ambiguity might be just enough to lead him to something important.

Or it might mean that he really didn't know anything.

Friday night and I was all dressed up with nowhere to go. I had shined my shoes, retrieved my blue suit from the cleaners, and unwrapped a Christmas tie. I could have used a haircut, and my knee felt warm to my touch—the throb in my slacks did not come from my groin—but I thought I deserved a break. My courtroom schedule unexpectedly had cleared, and my business still was slow enough that there was nothing pending that I couldn't put off for another month or two. That's what the death of a client will do.

For several months, the Dark Knight Lounge had promoted Friday as oldies night. A trio of mellow-sounding middle-aged Chicanos did the karaoke bit to almost every classic from the fifties and sixties, and a few from the seventies, for an appreciative audience who often found too many memories, or too many old lovers, deep in the smoky, cavernous corners of the Dark Knight. I guessed that the loud, drunken crowd offered what I needed to relieve the built-up melancholy that had started with Charlotte's death.

The neighborhood bar had enjoyed a renaissance of sorts. I could remember times when I was the sole customer, back in my harder-drinking days, before the knee. No one but me, my liquor and my buzz, and Vic, the bartender, who had called more cabs for me than anyone else in the world. In fact, he was the only person who had ever rolled me into the backseat of a taxi.

The Dark Knight was five minutes from my place, and as I drove around the block several times looking for a parking space, I promised myself that I would walk next time. Several young ladies, on their way inside, hopped and pranced under the yellow blinking lightbulbs that framed the door to the bar, and I instinctively thought it might be a good night for yours truly. I know, I know. I never learn.

When finally I limped past those same synchronous, nervous lights, I was elbow-to-elbow with what I estimated to be half of the Chicano professionals in the city, and an even greater percentage of men and women only a few weeks out of a halfway house. My kind of party.

The singers had refined their talents on the Eastside,

where they had grown up, and that right away meant a whole different attitude. They wiggled their butts, twirled their hands, and executed miniature pirouettes in more colorful clothes and shinier hair than Northside folks, but they were so well known that they did not offend anyone with the jive-ass, funky goose-stepping they had picked up from the brothers in the ghetto. Trio Bandido specialized in ancient rock and roll, before the Beatles even, and they more than ably belted out occasional *rancheras,* a blues song or two, and a bit of Patsy Cline, if the mood called for it. Always, before the night was finished, the mood called for all of it.

I'd stood at the bar for about a second when Vic stuck a long-neck in my hand then shouted over the din, "Yo, Louie, wassup?" I only nodded at him since words tended to evaporate in the Dark Knight's mix of thick smoke, strong perfume, and the sensual doo-wop of "Daddy's Home."

Abel Tapia nudged my arm.

"That was the theme song for the *pintos.* Guys telling their old ladies that they were coming back, someday. Hang tight, baby."

Between swallows of beer, I carried on a conversation that was only half heard by either one of us.

"It was a follow-up to 'Thousand Miles Away,' everyone knows that. Sounds right about prisoners and their women. Mood music from the joint. No wonder there are so many teary eyes in the house. Too much nostalgia. How's business, Abe?"

"Kind of slow. To be expected. Only been open for a few weeks. It'll come around. The people have to hear about us, then they'll start to rely on my place. That bit of excitement with that young guy, Valdez, actually turned out pretty good. Curiosity seekers came by, ended up buying something for dinner. Maybe I'll have that kind of entertainment on a regular basis."

He chuckled and I did not doubt that he knew the right kind of men to arrange a different show every time his bottom line edged a bit closer. Tapia had to have a street degree in Chicano marketing.

" 'Course, I ain't had the same kind of week as you. Heard about Weeds. What's up with that?"

He stared a little too intently at me, making me nervous, but I'm a jittery guy anyway. I had to sit down.

"Grab that booth, Abe. My knee gets tired easy."

He scooted across the floor and dumped himself into the booth before anyone else could claim it. He arranged a neat pile of empty beer bottles and overflowing ashtrays near the edge of the table. By the time I made it into my half of the booth, he had ordered two more beers.

He continued to stare at me, so I assumed that he had really wanted an answer to his question about my late client.

"The cops are looking into the hit-and-run. Could have been some drunk. It wasn't pretty."

"I heard he broke his neck and smashed open his head on the street. Bad way to go. Here's to Weeds. Rest in peace."

He raised his bottle and I mimicked his gesture, although I had no *sentimiento* for Lopez. I wondered why Abe Tapia, ex-con and current sole proprietor, even cared.

"How long you know Lopez?"

"A few years. In my other life. Lopez and I had a, a mutual friend, acquaintance. Part of maintaining in the city, you know how it is. You been on the Northside all your life, no? I lived around here only a few months."

There it was again. I had concluded that Lopez's penchant for "mutual" relationships had cost him a shattered skull, and now a guy who had about fifty different pictures carved into various sections of his skin had mentioned the same circumstance. An Aztec in a jaguar mask scowled at me from Tapia's forearm.

"This mutual acquaintance wasn't named Chick, by any chance?"

Tapia played with his beer bottle, tapped the table in time to Trio Bandido's version of Sunny Ozuna's greatest hit, "Talk to Me," and acted as though he was the only sentient being in the bar.

"Hey, Abe, you with me, man? You know Chick? Chick Montero?"

His fingers stopped their rhythmic beat. He stood up. He did not look at me as he talked.

"Sorry, Montez. It's an old habit. I'm not comfortable answering questions about people I know or don't know. Let me just say that if I knew anybody like Montero, a condition of me staying on the outside is that I wouldn't keep on knowing him, get it? Weeds should have wised up."

A huge hand slapped Tapia on the back. He flipped his head, turned slowly, and forced a wide grin to wrinkle his face.

"Hey, *cuñado.* Long time. What's happening?"

He strung out the words, and embraced a taller man wearing a suit. I did not recognize the stranger. Abe finally looked at me.

"I'm going to check out the place, Louie. Me and my bud here got some catching up to do. You be careful. The Northside's getting to be a dangerous place. But look who I'm talking to. Half the guys I bumped into in Cañon were your old clients. Hey, I mean it—thanks for bailing me out the other day. *Gracias.* "

He grabbed my hand and shook it quickly, then swaggered into the smoke, noise, and tension.

I waited for several minutes, reverting to my barfly role. Couples on the makeshift dance floor formed two lines and created what I thought were obscene versions of the stroll as the trio ended their set with a medley of Motown hits. As soon as they left the small stage, the jukebox blasted me with noise that I did not recognize. The waitress wanted to bring me another beer, but I turned her down. I was anxious to leave, but I didn't want to show it. The piece of paper Tapia had slipped into my hand had settled in my pants pocket like a sleepy snake. It was foolish, but I imagined that anyone in the Dark Knight could see its outline against my slacks. I walked with my hand next to my leg, pressed against my pocket.

I did not look at the paper until I was in my house, hunched over my desk.

Ask your poet pal about Montero.

Rad's voice came through loud and clear. He had called me from L.A. and I quickly gave him the dirt about my aborted excursion with oldies and Tapia. His excitement about my news was tangible enough to sail across the Southwest through the phone lines.

"That note means quite a few things, Louie."

"Yeah. Abe had it ready. He was expecting to run into me and he wanted to give me a message without anybody hearing him. That's number one."

He picked up my theme. "Number two is that he may be new in the neighborhood, but he knows about you and some of your old friends. Baca for sure."

"And number three must be that there's something that links Weeds Lopez and Charlotte Garcia."

Rad stopped me from going on with number three. "Whoa, Louie. Don't assume too much. There's something that links Baca and *Montero*. Could be as innocent as the fact that they both attended the same parochial grade school. But so far you got nothing that connects Lopez to Charlotte and the fire. Unless you haven't told me everything."

"You know everything I do. But it has to be Charlotte. Everybody knows I've been asking around about the fire. Tapia's one of those guys who understands paybacks and favors—he wanted to repay us for the timely foot you provided the other day, and so he thought he could give me a shove in a direction that might shake something loose. I got to talk with Baca again."

"Wait for me, Louie. I'll be back in Denver in a few days. Let me finish up here, then I'll see what I can do. It could be, you know, chancy."

"I'm in no hurry. I'll wait, but I'm going to keep on eye on Baca. Not that he's going anywhere. But what if he's the one on the spot? I wish I knew what the hell is going on."

"We'll know soon enough. Take it easy. Besides, I might have some news on Rachel. Patience, man. Just a few more days."

"I said I'm waiting. But that's only to talk with Baca about Montero. There are a few other things I can do."

"Did you get my package yet?"

"No. It'll probably show up tomorrow. I'll look it over, and then we can talk when you get in town. Easy."

The phone clicked off. I glanced at the note one more time, then folded it into my wallet. I thought it was safe.

11

◆

Concepción Sanchez hated his name. In sixteen years he hadn't been able to shake it. The best he could muster was Concep—not much, but he took it. Concep Sanchez beat up people who did not understand his prejudice against his mother's choice for his name, and so hardly anyone forgot and called him Concepción anymore, except his mother. As far as I knew, he hadn't punched her out.

I learned about Sanchez's identity quirks when I had to present to Judge Margaret Burgett a plausible hook as to why she shouldn't lock him up for several years as punishment for a severe bout of antisocial behavior. Something about a stolen car, a short but very high speed chase, and the little gangster's attempts at resisting arrest. His efforts got him a mauling from a pair of Denver cops. The judge put him away for a short stretch in Lookout Mountain, and that had been the last time I saw him until my promise to Bonnie Collins brought me back to Globeville.

The rec center was nothing more than flimsy wall dividers scattered around a hot, bright, and noisy concrete box. A basketball game rolled up and down the gym floor, creating all the sounds one would expect. A steady beat of shouting, huffing and puffing players mixed with athletic shoes squeaking against the hardwood, and the screech of a ref's whistle. Rap music floated above it all. I stood in the lobby outside the gym, surrounded by display cases filled with trophies, ribbons, and pictures of very serious looking baseball and basketball teams. All the players were Chicanos and the coaches were usually young white guys, except in the most recent photos. One coach had joined the staff and stayed. Because I had represented many of the kids who used his facilities, Sal Castro had arranged for Concep Sanchez to meet me at his center. There were no confrontations at Sal's place—no hassles—because Sal had worked that out when he first exhibited his toothy grin and *Indio* face at the gym and systematically dealt with the regulars—through various forms of persuasion. He kept the lid on with willpower and all that implied—including various forms of bribery and affection and, when needed, the force of his left hook and right jab. Although I did not see it, I knew his Golden Gloves trophy had a place of honor somewhere in the display case.

Before he agreed to get in the middle of Concep and me, he made me accept certain conditions.

"No cops. In fact, no one but you. Concep's been pushed around by the police already. He won't talk to you, or anyone, if he thinks you're with the cops. He knows you already, so I think he won't mind talking to you, for a short time. And you can't expect to use what he tells you, no way. The worst thing for him, the way he sees it, is that he gets tagged as some kind of squealer.

He talks to you and that ends it. No way he ever repeats anything in court. *¿Me entiendes?*"

"I don't expect him to rat off his friends. Just information, or rumor. He must have heard something."

"There are different ways to rat, Louie. Around here, it's a thin line between talking bullshit and talking too much."

"Hey, Louie, what's up? How's it hangin'?"

Neither Sal nor I had heard him approaching, and when he spoke we both twitched with the spasm of adult paranoia that came from too many headlines about juvenile killers—kids killing kids, actually. He stood in a shadow in a corner of the gray, dimly lit, institutional lobby.

I had to look up to talk to Concep Sanchez. He stood a good head taller than I, and twice as wide. Big-boned, pasty-faced, and thick in the neck—I always thought he was a bit thick in the brain, too.

"Hello, Concep. Been staying out of trouble? I haven't seen you in Judge Burgett's courtroom lately."

He stiffened, hunched his shoulders, and looked past me into the mortar joints of the rec center's walls. His T-shirt carried a public service message: D.A.R.E.—TO KEEP COPS OFF DONUTS.

"What's that? How come right away you got to dog me, talk that trash? Why you think you can come around here, actin' Hispanic, accusin' me of shit, and you don't even know, Montez? I ain't seen you for what, two, three years? Why I always got to be the accused? You're just as bad as the cops. Talkin' to me about every little fuckin' thing that goes down around here. I get hit up about some idiot tagger's mess, as if I was into that juvenile shit, and then that damn fire and shit. I give up."

"Yeah, I know, you're persecuted, Concep. It's rough.

I'm sorry—I forgot how sensitive you are."

His eyes moved from the walls to my face. They were buried deep among the years of whatever hell he had survived, whether created by himself or others it did not seem to matter right then.

Sal Castro moved around us, like a referee, sizing up the situation, but he did not speak, did not intercede. I took that to mean that I wasn't in too much heat, yet.

"So, what you want, Montez?"

"Anything about the fire. I know the cops have leaned on you and your friends, but that's not what's up with me. I'm working for Bonnie Collins, and Charlotte was a good friend, a good person. It's like a personal matter with me now. I got to level with you. I'm not saying I don't think it wasn't you or one of your crew. A person gets high, anything could happen—accidents happen all the time. Not much I can do about it. It's just that Bonnie and me, we need to know, that's all. It ain't much to ask—you know that."

The basketball game ended, the gym door crashed open, and a rush of sweaty young men swarmed around us. I could see that Sanchez was nervous. It probably did not do his reputation much good to be seen talking to me in a very hush-hush mode, especially with Sal on the perimeter. I waited until the crowd had thinned before I spoke again.

"It's not like I want you to snitch. All I need is a piece of information, if you got any, that will clear up whether there was a motive for what happened to Charlotte, or she was just in the wrong place at the wrong time. That's all."

Concep Sanchez moved closer. His smile did not reassure me.

"That's all? Shit, why don't you ask for one of my nuts. You're crazy if you think it ain't much, what you're askin'. I got my own problems and shit. I shouldn't be wastin' my time. But get this. None of us, none of the home boys, had any *pedo* with Charlotte, or that shack where she hung out. Mainly, none of that meant anything to any of us. I guess it's like this: If I wanted—*if*, I say— if I wanted to scare somebody off, for whatever *chingada,* and the person didn't get it, didn't listen, then I guess a fire in his face might make my point. And maybe the warning got carried away, and so somebody gets whacked. That's rough and shit. But I would think that the warning maybe made a few extra points, maybe got taken more serious. What you think?"

"A warning? About what? A warning to who? What is this, Concep?"

"Uh, I got to go, man. I been talkin' to you too long already. That's all I hear. It's not about anybody around here. Something else, somebody even out of the state. A guy I know was talked to about a favor for a friend of a friend, you know how that is. But that guy said *nel,* no way. Not for no fuckin' crumb cake from California. Later."

He sprinted from the building. Sal replaced him in the space next to my ear.

"He gave you more than I thought he would. Now what you going to do with it?"

"I have no idea, Sal. But I guess I got to talk to my friend from California."

"You got one, Louie?"

"I thought I did. And he's coming back to town in a matter of days. It's not what I thought I would hear. No way."

"That's the way it usually goes. When you least expect it. Ain't you used to that yet?"

"I'll never get used to learning things about my friends

that make me uncomfortable, make me doubt what they're all about. But you're right. That's the way it usually goes."

By the time I unlocked my front door and went through the motions of opening my office, I had almost reconciled myself to the fact that I still did not know very much about the young PI Conrad Valdez, except for the basics—a guess at his age, firsthand knowledge of his impressive self-defense skills, and the fact that he was from Los Angeles, as in California.

Rad's package turned out to be nothing more than a large manila envelope reinforced with mailing tape. I cut open one end and dumped the contents on my desk. Several photographs, newspaper articles, and typed pages of notes looked up at me. A yellow sheet from a legal pad framed Rad's handwriting and I read it first.

> *These come together after you read through them all. I think you should know this, just don't do anything with it until I'm back. Rachel's trail has gotten cold, so unless I learn something in L.A. I'll return to Denver by the weekend. Maybe we can dig something up on the fire. See you soon. RAD.*

I started with the pictures. Rad had collected images of a beautiful young girl—she had to be Rachel—in the company of the same group of other children, the Vargas kin in much younger days, I assumed, captured in typical family moments, romping around a picnic table or precariously balanced on a woebegone pony.

Rachel, the dark one, the Mexican daughter, stood out from the others, who could have walked off the set of *The*

Brady Bunch. They were kids, laughing, smiling, obviously spoiled and rich, but kids nevertheless. Except for Rachel. Her sensuality was evident even as a child, and in none of the photographs could I detect anything more than a forced smile, an automatic pose for a father/photographer who demanded that his subjects say "Cheese" for the camera.

Jaime, the eldest, towered over his brother and sisters. He looked to be in charge. In one picture, he held the reins of the pony while the anxious-looking Francisco and Patricia huddled on the oversized saddle and Rachel sat on the animal's rump. She did not look at the camera. Her stare focused on Jaime and I read too much into it. She was concerned that he would do something to the pony, something that would put her in harm's way. Or she was jealous of his authority. Why couldn't she lead the horse?

But when I quit tripping I realized that I saw nothing that triggered an explanation for Rachel's disappearance, or her infatuation with the legend of Oscar Acosta. Why did Rad think these Vargas memories were important? Why send them to me?

A newspaper article from the *L.A. Times* chronicled the latest trend in youth violence—the extensive use of fire as a weapon. Gangs had resorted to Molotovs and simple arson techniques to make their point, whether it was a warning to a potential witness or a signal to rivals that whatever truce had been in existence was now at an end. The article finished with the typical reference to the copycat nature of gangs and the ominous observation by the reporter that "soon gangs in Denver, Kansas City, and Dallas will follow the lead of their Los Angeles counterparts, and firebombs will light up the skylines of these urban centers as the deadly trend inexorably moves east."

Rad seemed to be telling me that the torching of the Keyhole could be simply part of the "deadly trend." My doubt remained. Even in L.A. the fires served a purpose, however warped. The only purpose for the fire I had heard of had come from the mumbled words of Concep Sanchez, and that involved Rad and a warning set up either by or for him. I didn't get it.

Rad had included a page from a collection of poetry. He had copied one of Charlotte's poems and circled a verse with red ink.

> *She knows what others never guess*
> *Pretending that it holds no power*
> *When love is not enough, our cold masks*
> *feed the energy*
> *That draws our screaming tears*
> *Painful faces in dark motion*
> *Have I earned the quiet of your threats?*

The poem was entitled *"Mi Compañera"*—My Companion. Rad had scribbled in the margin, *Bonnie = compañera?*

His remaining notes offered a concise summary of what he knew about the disappearance of Rachel. He had given me most of it when he had been in Denver, or over the phone since he had flown away to the Big Sky country. There was one page I had to read twice, just to make sure I understood what he had typed:

Rachel Vargas and Mel Kodiack planned to write a screenplay based on the life of Oscar Acosta. Kodiack confirmed that Rachel had submitted an outline to his (Kodiack's) agent, and that, after some editing by Kodiack, the agent had agreed to shop it around with his movie contacts. Kodiack had been upbeat about the project, and he fully expects a deal for the movie. Kodiack said, "The Acosta character fits into the current retro mood of a lot of people, especially the younger generation. This country may be screwed up because of what happened back then, in the sixties and seventies, the drugs, free love, rights for everyone and their mother, or this country may need a good dose of altruism and mau-mau confrontations again—either way you look at it, the legend of the Brown Buffalo has an audience just waiting for the story, and Rachel did a good job." Kodiack knew about Rachel's alleged contact with the missing Acosta, but he wasn't worried about it. "She's just into the character, into her story. It seems real to her. That happens to me with my books. It'll pass." Her disappearance troubled him, but he thought it might be just her "artistic tempera- ment." He promised to contact me if she got in touch with him.

All in all, Kodiack appeared to be dealing with the missing Rachel much better than Rad, as though he knew more about the quirks of the aspiring writer than her erstwhile friend and, I guessed, lover.

Or he could know the truth about the vanishing act, and so he wasn't worried. I wondered just how good Rad was at interviewing people. Did he know how to get at what he wanted, did he know how to use the person's words so that a fact, however small, was eventually turned loose, a fact that the person had no intention of ever divulging? I thought I knew how to do that, and that maybe I was the one who had to talk to Mel Kodiack. My years of cross-examining reluctant witnesses, from arresting police officers to hyperactive husbands, had to be good for something.

So one would think.

12

---◆---

I found Bonnie Collins at the Twentieth Street Gym. Charlotte had often expressed minor pride in the fact that Bonnie instructed an aerobics class twice a week during the lunch hour. "Not bad for an old lady, hey?"

I took a chance that it was her day to work her students.

The historic Twentieth had undergone a reconstruction and a resurrection. Near the U.S. Courthouse, it had never tried to be a fancy "fitness center," but it had provided the inner city with a place for some serious jock activity. The basketball games were still as intense as the pickup contests from years ago that had involved ex–Denver Nuggets and serious contenders from the semipros, but now the place catered even more to the downtown crowd— bankers and lawyers who pumped iron, government bureaucrats who jogged away their stress, and, in Bonnie's class, assorted professional women who sweated, groaned, and gyrated to her rigorous routines set against the music of everyone from Salt-N-Pepa to the Eagles.

I waited outside the aerobics room until the students filed out, wiping their bodies with towels, the Anglos flushed from their exertions, the Latinas and African-American women loud and energized. There were a couple of men in the class, both white, and they quickly disappeared into the bowels of the building. A small group of women stayed behind talking with Bonnie. She excused herself when she saw me in the doorway. A few of her students watched me, with curiosity I thought, but the rest hardly acknowledged my existence. I tried not to stare at the assorted shorts, spandex, and midriff-revealing abbreviated T-shirts.

"Want to sign up? You probably don't get much exercise."

Her face was red and glowing, and perspiration pasted her hair to the bony frame of her face.

"My leg, Bonnie. Can't do much with it the way it is. I barely managed to make it up the stairs. But I exercise—walking, that kind of thing. Even without a bullet in my knee I couldn't do what you put these people through."

"You'd pick it up quick. It's never too late to start working out. Ask your doctor. There must be something we can do, some kind of routine, that would be good for the leg and the rest of your body."

I tried to laugh off her wild suggestion. "Heh-heh. Sure, one of these days. Whenever the doc says it's a go. I'll call."

"So what you got, Louie? I hope it's good news. Must be something for you to stop by."

"It's kind of strange. This is my second visit to a gym in the space of two days. I haven't seen this much sweat since my older brother had to marry his first wife. But I thought you would want to know anything I've learned

106

about the fire. It's not much, but here it is."

She led me to a corner in the hall corridor where no one could eavesdrop without our seeing them. First, I handed her Rad's copied page of Charlotte's poetry.

She scanned it, focused on the marked verse for a minute, then handed it back to me.

"That was in a collection called *No Boundaries Except Our Own*. '*Mi Compañera*' is about our relationship, and, yes, she was writing about me. But that verse is a tiny piece of a much longer work. You should read the whole thing. Most of it is about the good times we had. It's honest—too honest for me. I never liked it all that much, but Charlotte thought it was one of her best. What does it have to do with anything?"

"Rad sent it to me, with a question mark. She wrote about threats, and that could be taken several ways. How old is the poem?"

"I don't like this. Why are you doing this? You can't think that I had—"

"Easy, Bonnie."

I wanted to step closer to her, maybe try a hug, to let her know that I meant no harm, that I had no suspicions of her, but I wasn't sure how she would take such a gesture from me. I didn't move.

"I'm just giving you everything I know. Rad had a question—the verse raises obvious questions, simply because of the threat imagery. That's all. Rad wouldn't be a very good detective if he didn't follow up on something like this. Threats can mean anything—threats to leave, to break off the relationship, threats about another person—hell, anything at all."

Her eyebrows arched when I said the bit about another person, but then her face relaxed and I could see that she wanted to believe me.

"That's right. And that's how Charlotte meant those words. She wrote about a difficult time we were having as a couple. We were threatened by many things, but nothing physical, nothing related to the kind of violence that took her life. It was more that we were threatened with the end of our love, and she tried to put that in the poem. It wasn't a love poem, it was a poem about life— our life together. But, like I said, I didn't care for it all that much. She did better work. She wrote it almost seven years ago. If your friend thinks it means anything connected to the fire, tell him he's grasping at straws. And tell him I don't appreciate it."

"Fair enough. I'll pass it on to him. He's flying in tonight. He also sent me this story about gang-related fires. You can keep that. I've got another copy."

She nodded and stuffed the page into her gym bag.

"But the real piece of news is that I talked with Concep Sanchez."

"I thought you would. The cops talked to him, too. It wasn't him. He and Charlotte related to each other, at a certain level. That neighborhood was Charlotte's home, remember. She grew up a few blocks from the Keyhole. She told me once that she saw a little bit of herself in the kids, including Concep. That's the way she was."

She stopped, abruptly, and that was my cue to continue before she would have to excuse herself so she wouldn't feel embarrassed about the loneliness that was about ready to stream down her face.

"From what he said, there definitely was a message tied to the fire, but it couldn't have been anything related to Charlotte. According to Concep, it was something else—somebody else entirely—who was supposed to be warned about staying out of another person's business.

It had nothing at all to do with Charlotte—if we can believe Concep."

Bonnie expelled the breath she had been keeping in behind her pursed lips. A quirky look shadowed her blood-infused face, something between relief and resignation.

She almost whispered, "Do you know who or what? *Any* possible link to Charlotte?"

I did not want to implicate Rad without more, and I still did not understand what it was that I would have implicated him in, except that an allusion to a "crumb cake from California" had fallen quickly from the lips of Globeville's teenaged criminal-in-residence.

"He, uh, didn't explain much. Just that the fire was meant to warn somebody off, and that Charlotte's death wasn't part of the plan. I'm sorry, Bonnie, but I think it's all we probably will get, until the cops finally arrest somebody for the firebombing. But it's more than you had."

"Yeah. You're right. And at least it is something. Thank you, Louie. I better go. I'm starting to get chilled out here. Thanks."

She rushed off in the general direction of the stairs to the showers, and I left the building. The downtown public gym had provided a place for the stretching, rolling, and pounding of the muscles and ligaments of every variety of citizen over the decades of its existence, but it had never seen Luis Montez work up a sweat within the confines of its walls. That is, until that day when I talked to Bonnie Collins about her dead companion and failed to bring up my incriminated friend. Drops of moisture rolled underneath my white dress shirt and into the waistband of my boxers. My knee creaked as I limped down the stairs and out the door into the heavy summer air of

Twentieth Street in downtown Denver. I took a deep breath of afternoon city dust and tried to clear my conscience.

I decided that I wanted to eat lunch, and because I seemed to be surrounded by a good health milieu, I opted for fried chicken from Hot Rodney's in Five Points, a few minutes from the gym. I rationalized that Rodney's spicy chicken may have been dripping with grease and hot sauce, but at least it wasn't red meat. I could pass on the coleslaw and potato salad and do that much more for my arteries. A beer would be nice.

Rodney Harrison had tried to kill me once. Later, I could see how he might have thought he had justification. At the time, it was a night that lasted a lot longer than the hangover.

I had represented the mother of a pair of his children and convinced a county court judge that Rodney needed to be restrained from ever setting foot in their comfortable ranch-style house along Martin Luther King Boulevard, a mile or so west of Stapleton International Airport. For some reason, he had copped a very bad attitude about me and my role in the breakup of his family. As luck would have it, my luck of course, shortly afterward we ran into each other during one of those nights when Jim Beam played both ends against the middle. Before we were through we each had spent time sobering up in the drunk tank. After that, it was like in the movies—one of those buddy movies. We realized we had more in common than just a fine and time served for disorderly conduct.

Every few months I dropped by to eat his food and, in his own special way, he pitched in when I needed a process server who wasn't afraid of bikers and their dogs, or who could retrieve a child-support check from a late-paying respondent for one of my clients and not take no for an answer. We never talked about Evelyn, his ex.

There were about thirty people in the small café and bar that couldn't have held Snow White and her Seven Dwarfs, and, except for me, they were all black, they all smoked, and everyone had a plate in front of him or her piled high with chicken, ribs, or hot links. Outdated calendars broke up the monotony of grease stains on the walls. The overriding theme of the pictures was sultry, ebony women in high fashion. In the background, almost lost in the din, Billie Holiday and Lester Young traded their respective tragedies.

I nudged my way to the counter and caught the attention of the young woman taking orders. I hollered out, "Number One and a Bud." She nodded in between ringing up the cash register, making change, and handing out platters of food that were shoved to her by hands that reached out through the glassless window in the wall that separated the front from the kitchen.

Rodney was in the kitchen, and when I had my beer in my hands I peeked in through the window.

"Hey Rodney! Give me a minute when you can."

A tall, muscular man with gray grizzle on his chin and a splotched apron around his waist looked up from a tray of bubbling grease. He worked his face into an acknowledgment of my greeting and then grabbed another tray covered with pieces of chicken dipped in his mysterious batter. I made my way to the back of the room and waited for my food and Rodney.

By the time he made it to my corner, a pile of chicken bones was all that remained of my meal, Magic Sam had replaced Lady Day and Prez, and I was well into my third beer. Rodney's hot sauce encouraged the alcoholic in all of his customers.

"How's the leg, Montez? Still gimping around, looking for sympathy from all the young senoritas? What an example of an officer of the court! You get in more heat than the birds in my kitchen. And how can you drink all this beer and eat all that food? Why ain't you fat like all the other lawyers that come in here?"

He gathered up my empties and my limp paper plate and dumped them in a nearby trash can. Then he set down his own beer on the tiny table that had room for maybe one more bottle. I hadn't been this close to Rodney Harrison since he and I were too angry to compromise with each other and too drunk to really hurt ourselves and I had had to twist a straight razor out of his hand. No guns for Rodney; he was old school.

"I live right, you know that. Hell, man, I just left the gym. How many people come in here and can say that? I deserve a good meal"—he started to smile in appreciation—"but I settled for some of your greasy roadkill because I need to talk to you, maybe ask for your advice."

"You got your whatever. Those bones I just trashed were smoother than Michael Jordan's head on game night. You can't live without my chicken. We both know that. What you want?"

"I suppose you heard about Weeds."

"Oh yeah. Outside your house, wasn't it? Hit-and-run was what I read in the papers. That guy was what we used to call a weasel. They got better names nowadays. What's your interest in Weeds? You in a jam over that now?"

"No, no. Nothing like that. Wilson Lopez was my client. Still is my client. There's a good chance that a guy he owed money to had him splattered all over my front lawn, and I want to know if that's true or not. He wasn't my favorite client, but you know how it is."

"Sorry, Louie, I don't. Must be hard to maintain an attorney-client relationship with a corpse. You don't owe anything to that guy. But that's your business. What you think I can do?"

"This may sound like it's coming from left field, but you run into all kinds of people—you knew Weeds. If anybody might have heard about his affairs, his street action, I thought it would be you."

He shrugged his shoulders but he knew I was right. Rodney had been my source for information many times in the past. It must have been his sauce—it made people open up to him. Sometimes I thought I should have a bottle of the fiery stuff in my office and use it whenever I was having a particularly tough deposition with a recalcitrant witness—what an interesting way to practice law.

I followed up on the shrug with my question.

"Can you think of any tie-up between Weeds, Chick Montero, and a dude named Bobby Baca? You know anything about that?"

He studied the label on his beer and I guess he was having a hard time making out the words because he didn't say anything for what seemed like several minutes. I've had the same problem, at other times, so I did not rush him for an answer.

Finally Rodney Harrison said, "Denver's supposed to be world class now. We got a baseball team and almost a new airport and light rail and all kinds of upscale improvements. And yet it's still a cow town, still just a small, almost hick town. If I'm lying, I'm flying. Seems everybody knows everybody else, even if you don't want to. Funny that you should ask about Chick Montero. We don't get along."

"I'm not surprised. He doesn't appear to have many friends."

"Tell me about it. He tried to muscle some money out of me a while back—the usual bullshit, under the name of insurance. Said he had a business partner that could take care of any problems I might have—you've heard that one before. Anyway, I brushed him off, and he hasn't been back, but right after that a guy came around looking for him, another Chicano guy. You Mexicans ain't nothing but trouble for me, you know that? He said he heard that Montero had been around, and he wondered if I knew how to get in touch with him. I brushed that guy off, too."

"Did this other Chicano give you a name?"

"It wasn't that kind of visit."

"Anything unusual about him? Tattoos, scars? Maybe carried a computer case?"

He thought a minute.

"No, nothing like that. He toted a notebook, that was about it. When he started to leave, he dropped it, and all these pages fell out. They looked like poems, I kid you not. But I doubt that anybody who reads poetry would be looking for Chick Montero, especially with the tone of voice that guy used. But it was nothing. I haven't seen Montero for weeks. He hasn't been back. I think he knows better. This really ain't his neighborhood."

I looked around the place and had to agree. Hot Rodney's did not seem right for a Northside extortion artist, or for a Globeville poet. But then I had to think again. I doubted that anybody in the world would ever associate the Five Points chicken shack with the world-famous Luis Montez, Esq., and yet the pieces of gristle stuck between my teeth and the sticky remnants of hot sauce on my fingers did not lie. In fact, it came off as fairly natural, once I thought about it over a couple more beers and another of Rodney's music tapes.

13

$\blacklozenge$

Rad's return started out quietly. It was late, after nine, when the phone rang, but I still hovered, a bit lethargically, behind the beer and chicken from Rodney's. I hadn't been able to get much done after my talk with the soul food chef, but I had hung around my office for appearance' sake. Of course my office also was my house, so it wasn't all that difficult.

After some small talk with Rad, I made a suggestion.

"I'll come by around ten, okay? We can get a drink, or a bite if you're hungry. Then we can go over what we know."

"Fine with me. We'll be in the hotel bar."

I showered and changed my clothes. I read his notes again, looked at the pictures, then played back in my head my conversations with Bonnie, Rodney, and Concep Sanchez. There must have been an instant when I wondered what Rad meant by "we."

I had wanted only to resurrect my law practice, to get

back in the good graces of paying clients and patient judges and honorable opposing counsel. I had wanted only to get on with my life, and, in my own way, that's what I was doing. It just seemed a little more complicated than usual.

Rad Valdez had come to town looking for the missing girl, Rachel Espinoza/Vargas, whom he wanted to marry, and about whom all I knew was that her sensuality had overshadowed a rather spectacular beach and ocean, and that she had concocted a crazy story about an over-the-edge, missing (long dead) Chicano writer. Concep Sanchez, who, for a number of diverse and sometimes legitimate reasons, could not manage to take care of his teenaged wife and infant daughter, but who had a certain authority in matters of the street, had planted a seed of doubt in my head about Rad. Now it appeared that Rad's presence in town had something to do with the fire that had claimed the life of Charlotte Garcia. And somewhere in all that, I had to sort out the killing of my client Wilson Lopez, and the unlikely linkage between the poet Bobby Baca and the small-time hood Chick Montero.

There was something else, but I could not put my finger on it. Something showed up on my internal radar like a glowing blip, but that was all I picked up. No definition, no details. Only that pulsating blip and a strong intuition that when I learned what it meant, I might have already crashed into the side of the mountain.

When I finally left to pick up Rad, the unexpectedly cool night air hit my face like a slap from an insulted barmaid and I assured myself that it felt good. It might keep me sharp.

Rad had changed work stations from his first visit. He had checked into one of Denver's oldest and poshest downtown hotels, and I had to marvel at the apparent magnitude of his expense account. Old man Vargas may have been loaded, but I thought that even he had to have placed some limits on how much he was willing to spend to keep his private investigator comfortable. Maybe money was no object in the search for his missing daughter.

The bar had a good-sized crowd, and I was a bit surprised. I had never enjoyed downtown hotel bars all that much. First, there were few Chicanos, if any, in these kinds of places, unless the hotel's kitchen crew stopped by for a couple of cool ones after the dining room closed. And the bartenders usually intimated that they knew I wasn't a paying guest, and so that made me less interesting.

I had to doubt my own motives whenever I did find myself sipping an overpriced draft in one of the saloons that fancied dark wood and subdued chandeliers. Why would a local hang out in a bar designed for transients, well-heeled transients, granted, but even so, people who were supposed to move on after a day or two of business meetings or a couple of nights of tourist fun? I either had to lead a rather boring life or I was a hustler. Con men and prostitutes hung out in hotel bars, elbow-to-elbow with the registered customers—at least that had been my assumption.

Rad sat in a booth along a wall, and sitting across from him was an older man. I immediately recognized Oscar Vargas from the pictures Rad had sent me. Even though he was several years older than when he had been captured in the few snapshots of family interaction that I had been privileged to view, there was no mistaking him—he looked extremely good for someone who had to be in his late sixties, at least. I gave him a quick once-over—well-tanned, still trim, with defined, almost sculptured features, and a thick head of totally silver hair that flowed in a thick wave back across his head and onto the collar of his designer-label knit shirt. The image worked and I took it for granted that the guy definitely was not nouveau riche—just riche.

"Louie, meet Oscar Vargas. Mr. Vargas, the man I told you about, Luis Montez."

He shook my hand and made a gesture for me to sit down. I squeezed in next to Rad.

"At last, Mr. Montez. Conrad has been keeping me up to date on his search for Rachel, of course, and your name has been mentioned more than once. That ugly encounter with those holdup men, and then that strange incident with the missing manuscript and the broken file cabinet. And of course, your close call in that fire. I'm not sure if it's just young Conrad's impetuous nature or *your* lifestyle—but whatever, it seems that you two have been having quite a time together."

I looked around for a waitress and caught the eye of a plump brunette who almost immediately appeared at my side. I ordered a beer and asked the others if they wanted something. They declined my offer. Two full pot-bellied glasses of amber liquor sat in front of Rad and Vargas.

"Yeah, Rad and I have had some fun. That's for sure. How's the search going?"

Rad started to explain but he was interrupted by Vargas.

"Not good, not good at all, in my opinion. Rachel's been missing for a month, and still nothing's turned up. That's why Jaime and I decided to meet Conrad here in Denver, so that we could be closer to what's going on."

"You and your son came out here just to listen to Rad and me talk over his search?"

He glanced at Rad and then quickly responded.

"Well, not completely. We were in Dallas—business. Rather than return directly to L.A., we coordinated with Conrad, and so we can spend a few days here, helping out, I hope. We won't get in the way."

"Yes, Louie," Rad added. "They called me when I was still in Montana and said they wanted to go over what I had turned up, if anything. Denver seemed like a convenient place to do it. I thought your perspective would be beneficial. As soon as Jaime joins us, we can get into it."

I nodded. I would pretend that it sounded sensible if that was what everybody wanted. The concerned family obviously should hear firsthand what Rad was thinking, and Rad probably thought I could add some balance. The truth was, though, I did not know anything about Rachel's disappearance that the Vargas men would want to hear. They could have met in L.A., but I guessed it was easier for everyone to gravitate to Denver, especially if Vargas was on his way back to California from Texas.

We waited for Jaime by going over the things about Rad's investigation that we assumed all of us already knew. We were still waiting a quarter of an hour later, so the ebb-and-flow of feeling each other out started. Mr. Vargas and Rad did not want to proceed without the eldest son, and I was willing to accept that, too. It must have been tradition. In my own family, if something important was discussed, we had to hear what Jesús, Jr., had to say before we could proceed. As long as we could find good old Chuey, of course.

Oscar Vargas asked, "How long have you lived in Colorado? It's a beautiful state. Some of it reminds me of California, when I was a boy. Many years ago. Maybe I'll look into buying some land up in the mountains."

"I'm a native. My mother was born here, too, in a mining town that no longer exists. My father came up from Zacatecas when he was a young man. Now my brothers and sisters are spread out over the Southwest. I think Colorado is beautiful, too. But it's much too crowded. Too many immigrants."

"How can you say that? Your father—"

"Oh, I don't mean Mexicans. There are too many damn Californians and Texans moving into the state. You know how that is. You've seen what happened to your state over the past couple of decades. Too many people, wouldn't you agree?"

It's not like I really gave a damn. I hadn't noticed an overwhelming influx of displaced Simi Valley refugees into the Northside. But I said it to get a rise out of the old man and he obliged, in his own civilized way. Vargas pulled on the cuff of his shirt and quietly cleared his throat. He took a healthy gulp of his drink.

He said, "You just told me to keep out of your state. Not in an impolite manner, but still. I guess I'll have to reconsider my plans."

Then he let it go. I played with the idea of baiting him some more, don't ask me why. I react that way to money, sometimes. It's my own little version of the class struggle. Childish, yes, but some people say I never quite grew up anyway. My father says that.

Rad probably read my mind. He squirmed in the booth and coughed. He quickly steered the subject back to Rachel.

Rad had contacted Brian Gulf, the screenwriter in Rachel's condo group, and had concluded that the guy did not know anything about Rachel's whereabouts.

"He was half drunk when I talked with him and, from what I heard from an actor friend, he's pretty much washed up because of the booze. He babbled about how he had tried to write while in Mexico but I got the impression that he didn't get much done. He apparently gave it up and flew back and was on a bender for about a week. He had credit card receipts from about fifty different bars and liquor stores, all during the time when Rachel was still in Los Cabos, and then when she disappeared. Claimed that he hardly knew Rachel. He was there at the invitation of Mel Kodiack, an old friend, and he said he didn't really see much of Rachel. If he had been a bit more in control of himself, he might have given me a lead, or I might even consider him a suspect. But I doubt it."

Oscar Vargas nodded. "I've asked around about Gulf, and I agree with your assessment, Conrad. His writing career is finished, at least with the movie people. They don't care about the drinking, of course. He just doesn't produce. He doesn't have it anymore. That doesn't mean he wouldn't do something to harm Rachel, but I don't see any connection. There's been no ransom demand. If anyone harmed Rachel, and that was it only, I think we would have heard something, found some trace. She's just disappeared. Brian Gulf doesn't seem to be the type who could pull off something like that."

He raised his hand and waved at a man who had entered the bar while he was talking. The man wore a dark blazer over a shirt similar to Oscar's, and he had the same full head of hair, although his was completely black, and before we were introduced it was obvious that Jaime Vargas had finally made it to what had turned out to be a meeting about his missing sister. My only surprise was that next to him stood a petite, younger female version of Jaime—Patricia—who had not been referred to by the father or Rad.

Patricia's brown leather bomber jacket seemed inconsistent with the recent warm weather, but when she sat down and removed it I had to rethink my theory. A thin, sleeveless, bright pink T-shirt clung to her lean torso, and in the air-conditioned bar, goose bumps quickly popped out on her arms. Other than that, she appeared to be unaffected by the atmosphere or the company in the booth.

Introductions were made again, and this time Jaime's businesslike abruptness contrasted sharply with his sister's timid and bored mien. Jaime quickly took over the conversation.

"Although I am sure that Rachel is okay, I suppose we have to let this latest episode of hers run its course. So we are very interested in what happened to Rachel's manuscript, Mr. Montez. There doesn't seem to be any reason for it, and yet, it must have something to do with her disappearance. Is there anything you can remember about it, anything at all? You must have read it. You are the only person we can turn to on this. You had the book. I'm not sure anyone else saw the version you did. Is there anything?"

His brisk tone and rather direct manner had unsettled me. I never have liked that thin line between taking care of business and acting like a jerk. Jaime impressed me as one who easily blurred that distinction.

They all looked at me except for Patricia, who sat outside the booth, on a chair in the way of the bar's employees. She had more interest in her drink than anything I might say.

Because it was my turn to tap-dance, I said, "I leafed through the book, that's all. There wasn't anything unusual, that I noticed. It was a pretty straightforward suspense novel, about a man's murder. It wasn't that interesting, if you want to know the truth."

Rad added, "I've read her book, too. Louie's right. I didn't see anything in it. We can guess all night, but I doubt we will hit on why it was taken from Louie's office."

Jaime Vargas nodded almost simultaneously with his father. They agreed with Rad. I was about to say something when Patricia surprised us all and interrupted. Her high-pitched, reedy voice broke and squeaked on her words.

"Shouldn't you be trying to find this Acosta guy? What have you found out about him? That must have something to do with Rache's trip."

She called her adopted sister Rache, and the disappearance a "trip." Those things stuck with me.

Oscar Vargas rushed in after Patricia quit speaking. "She's right. What have you on that, Conrad?"

"Nothing, I'm afraid. I've learned plenty about the real Oscar Acosta, but he's long dead, unheard of since nineteen seventy-four, except for some unsubstantiated sightings that seem to have more to do with mystical longing than fact. Whoever had been talking to Rachel wasn't the real Acosta, of course, but I don't have anything on who could have been leading her on like that. Nothing, yet."

"And you won't learn anything about him. You're looking in the wrong places! You can't do this, Conrad, you know it. Oh, it's all a mistake, all . . ."

Patricia's outburst had definitely caught me off guard.

She did not finish. She awkwardly pushed her way out of her chair. The senior Vargas attempted to grab her arm but he was too slow. He shouted, "Patricia!" She looked at him for the briefest instant and then practically hurled herself out of the bar.

I leaned into Rad and asked, "What the hell?"

He shook his head, then said, "Find her, Louie. Talk

to her. Calm her down. I'll wait for you here." The other men agreed with their eyes.

I did as I was told. Rad *was* the professional investigator, after all, and Patricia's rather theatrical exit had tweaked my interest—just a bit.

As I tried to catch up with Patricia, who had dashed through the revolving door at the front of the hotel, I puzzled over why I kept getting these really bad feelings about my young friend, and why his name came up more and more in the company of generally negative vibrations, and when would I get to talk with Rad alone. But as I gamely made my way down the dark, almost deserted city street and my knee groaned in protest, most of all I wondered why the guy with the bad leg had to be the one to run after the young woman with the fat-free frame and an apparently healthy dose of adrenaline.

14

◆

The coolness I had noticed earlier had eased into a hint of wet, even cooler weather, and my leg felt especially stiff. For several minutes I limped around the late-night Denver streets, looking for the runaway waif with a propensity for spontaneity. I doubted that I could talk her into doing anything reasonable but there was a chance that she would be safer—a bit, anyway—if I, if anyone, was with her. Patricia Vargas did not inspire confidence that she was an independent, self-reliant young woman with a cool and sober head on her angle-iron shoulders. Those are not the kind of women I normally end up chasing down a dark Denver avenue.

Near the Sixteenth Street Mall, under a streetlight that during the day served as a marker for a vendor who blared Mozart over the heads of his lunchtime customers as they queued up for fifty-cent hot dogs, Patricia's outline drew me to her like a magnet of disappointment. She stood next to a newspaper vending machine, huddled around it as though it offered a source of heat. I tried to be graceful as I walked toward her. If she decided to take off again I was not going to chase her—it would do neither of us any good, particularly my leg, and I wasn't in the mood anymore, anyway. I was starting to resent the Vargas clan.

She watched me approach, her eyes wary but tired. Whatever she had been on was starting to wear off; whether it was fear or drugs I had not yet concluded.

"Patricia, I know you're upset about your sister, but try to think this through. Come back—we can all talk about anything that's bothering you."

"Oh, hell yes. You must think I'm a real idiot. I'm sorry, but I can't, I just can't."

Her thin frame trembled and shook, and what little color her face held vanished. She lurched against the newspaper rack and out into the street. I grabbed her as she fell, and prevented her fragile-looking body from smashing into the asphalt. She was out. It took a few minutes, which surprised me because she did not weigh that much, but I finally moved her from the street and up against the side of a bank building. I hoped that Rad or one of her relatives would show up and take her off my hands. I didn't know what to do with her. I didn't want to leave her, but there did not seem to be anything else I could do. I had to get her some assistance.

In the distance, an ambulance wailed on its way to the emergency room. A few blocks over, a bit of late-night traffic moved slowly through downtown. I felt incredibly alone.

I rubbed her arms and hands, trying to stimulate some reaction so that she would wake up and I could get on with whatever it was I had to do that night. I knew I should not be baby-sitting a hysterical young woman

126

who had literally fainted in my arms. I knew I did not want to explain the situation to anyone else—I had to get her to come to before a cruising cop made the evening even more disagreeable, even though I was completely innocent, even though all I was doing was trying to be a good guy. These things never worked out for me, that I knew.

"Oh-h-h. What the . . ."

She groaned and moved around. She tore away from me when she focused on my face. I did my best to reassure her.

"Hey, hey, it's me. Montez. I was talking to you back at the hotel. You and your family. About your sister. Are you okay?"

She sat up and I moved a step back from her. She grimaced and covered her mouth with fluttering fingers. I thought she was going to lose it, but she took a few deep breaths and finally her jaw muscles relaxed.

"Yes, yes. I remember. I'm sorry. I get all worked up about Rachel, and everything. I guess I was woozy from not eating. I haven't been eating right. I'm sorry. I'll be all right. I just need a place to sleep. Maybe a room around here. I don't know, I just don't know."

She faded in and out and her words trailed off into that darkness of her mind where I did not want to wander. I told her that we should return to her father and brother, but that only caused her to tense up again. Quickly I said that there was no rush.

She said, "Jaime, Rache . . ." then was silent for a few minutes. I squatted next to her trying my best to put a good face on the circumstances, still hoping that I could get her back to the hotel where I could extricate myself from any more involvement. And then, unexpectedly, her eyes opened wide and something like clarity shone through her pupils. She had returned, however briefly I could not tell, but I took advantage of her seemingly restored state of mind.

"I promise everything will be fine. Your family must be worried."

Almost serenely, she responded, "I can't go back. Can we go somewhere else? I just need some time to myself. Some time to think. Maybe I should just go, and find somewhere I can stay."

"That's not a good idea. Let's return to your father. He'll be worried. We have to tell him that you are all right. Come on, let's go."

Her agitation returned. "No! Leave me alone! You can take off. I need some time! Leave me alone!"

She shouted and her voice echoed among the buildings and empty parking lots.

"Okay, okay. Calm down. I won't make you do anything you don't want to do. But you can't just go off into the night. Maybe I should call someone."

She wasn't buying it. That bit of clarity I had noticed only a few seconds before was rapidly dimming and it was easy for me to see that she was about ready to run again. My head carried me on that trip until I saw old man Vargas and his surly son pointing their fingers at me, accusing me of losing another one of the Vargas women—what was it with me and the Vargas women, anyhow? I stopped it as soon as I could. I was not going to let that happen.

"Let me take you to my father's house. You can get something to eat there, and you can be alone, if you want. But don't run off. Please, don't."

Dumping the inconvenient Patricia Vargas on Jesús was all I could come up with at that point. I did not think it was smart to be alone with her, so I ruled out taking her to my place. My father's house seemed safe, for all of us, and from there I could call Rad and let him know what had happened. Patricia was afraid of something, and she refused to deal with it with her father, her brother, or her sister's closest friend. Somehow that left me, and, now, my cranky and sure to be mad-about-being-disturbed-in-the-middle-of-the-night father.

None of this was what I had planned for the evening, but a short time after Patricia had fallen into my arms we climbed into my car and I drove her into the Westside. We stopped in front of my father's small but neat house. She looked it over for a long time, then she nodded and said, "Okay."

And so Patricia Vargas moved into the home of Jesús Genaro Montez.

"Rache was crazy. You know that, don't you?"

Patricia used her fork to push the remnants of an omelette around her plate. Jesús had thrown together a midnight meal for the gaunt young woman who had shown up at his front door whimpering and shaking like a drenched puppy. The old man never had a chance. With me, he was angry. With her, he took pity and immediately tried to fatten her up. He whipped eggs, cheese, onion, tomatoes, green peppers, and garlic powder into a froth and then warmed up a plate of fried potatoes left over from his own dinner that he had stored in his refrigerator. He apologized for not having any beans handy. Then he proudly served his meal with red chile, tortillas, coffee, and juice. I was not given a plate.

I thought about reminding him that he had never fed me in such a grand manner, not in the almost five decades that we had known each other. But my hands were full dealing with Patricia. She was such a basket case that I had trouble trying to keep her on the same planet as me.

I poured myself a cup of coffee and gagged. My father could not make a decent pot of coffee even if Juan Valdez guided him step by step.

"That's a hard thing to say about your own sister. Why crazy?"

She made me nervous just sitting in her chair. Her eyes darted around the room, her foot tapped an incessant tempo on the linoleum floor, and every few minutes when her upper lip twitched and arched she would casually flick at her mouth with her fingers as though a bothersome gnat had landed on a tooth.

She said, "Hah! How can you say that? She's gone, ain't she? What else you need?"

That stumped me. Maybe she was right. I just could not see it. I was either too dense, or I needed several of those dark drinks that old man Vargas and Rad had sipped at the hotel. The liquid that my father called coffee would have to suffice.

Jesús ambled to the refrigerator and opened the freezer compartment drawer. He took out a box of chocolate-covered cherries. Quite ceremoniously, he opened the box, held a paper towel on the candies, and shook it over his sink. Tiny black dots fell into the sink. My father and the whacked-out young Californian had joined forces in a wild conspiracy to rob me of whatever small bit of sanity I still retained.

"Dad, what the hell are you doing?"

"Dessert, as soon as Ms. Vargas finishes. It should be obvious."

"What was that in the sink? And why did you freeze these things?"

Patricia flinched suddenly, then stood up.

"Where's the bathroom? I need to use it."

Jesús escorted her to the right place. When he returned, I repeated my questions.

"That old lady from across the street, Germaine, gave me these, said her grandkids gave them to her but she can't eat so much sweet stuff. Between you and me I think she's a little late worrying about her figure. Anyway, I had the box on my table. Ants found them, and there was a string of insects from outside into my kitchen. I did what I could to the parade, but some had made it into the box. All this sugar drove the *hormigas* crazy. But they couldn't get to the cherries. Must have pissed them off to be so close and yet still out of reach. Each one is wrapped in foil. See?"

He picked up one of the candies and unwrapped it, then popped it into his mouth.

"You froze the candy to kill the ants? You didn't do that, did you?"

He moved the solid piece of chocolate, fruit, and sugar around his jaw like a marble. In between slurps, he mumbled, "Ga, uh, there were uh, a, a few ants in the box, so I, ga, uh, zapped them in the freezer. The candy's still good. Here, uh, try one."

The sounds of Patricia vomiting in my father's toilet stopped us both.

I wanted to say that I hoped Patricia's reaction had nothing to do with his cooking, but I restrained myself.

Jesús said, "No wonder she's so skinny. She doesn't keep her food down, Louie. *¿Cómo se dice,* bull ick, *o qué?*"

"Bulimia. I should have guessed. Her fingernails are discolored and her teeth are bad. What a family!"

My father and I looked at each other and passed what must have been a private signal to act as though we had

131

heard nothing, because when Patricia returned, that is exactly what we did. Neither one of us commented on her disturbing after-meal routine, but we both had lost our appetites. She was subdued and quieter now. She asked for a glass of water, then started talking again about her sister.

"Rache has always been on the edge, ready to crack. She's adopted, you know. We all knew, even her."

I asked, "How did that change anything? So what if she was adopted?"

She shrugged her shoulders, causing the thin bones of her upper torso to wiggle beneath the pink T-shirt. Her frail body had to lack the strength necessary to support the worries and torments that she so blatantly exhibited. She was a wounded animal begging for comfort, or a mercy bullet.

Finally, she answered, "It didn't mean that much to my brothers or me, but she always thought we treated her like something less, not an equal. But that wasn't true. Mom and Dad gave her everything they gave us, sometimes more—just to show her that she was completely a part of the family, I guess. And Jaime—man! He spoiled her rotten. But Rache let the adoption thing get to her anyway. She tried harder than any of us to really get out from under the thumb of Dad—that's the way she put it—but still she never turned down her monthly allowance. She took advantage of the Vargas name, but then she would do anything she could to embarrass us. When you get down to it, she only wanted to be one of us, really one of us. The sad part is that she was. She just didn't know what to do with it."

Jesús decided he should say something.

"But why would she deliberately disappear? Your father must be sick with worry, and you are too, I can tell.

You think something bad has happened to her, something that maybe she didn't expect."

I said, probably too anxiously, "Is that true, Patricia? Do you know something about Rachel's sudden departure from Mexico? The missing manuscript, and this man calling himself Oscar Acosta? What do you know about all that?"

Her mouth twitched again but she ignored it. I thought I could see the beginnings of tears forming in the corners of her eyes, and she had to clear her throat before she could speak.

"Of course I'm worried. She's my sister! No matter what she thinks, we all love her, all of us, even Jaime. She's our sister. Oh God! Where is she? I love her, I do, I do."

She had ignored my questions. Her words had turned into screeches and finally she quit talking. At last the tears ran down her face. She broke down and my father and I let her go with it. She cried and sobbed, and repeated Rachel's name, and once or twice she mumbled, "Just come home, Rache, just come home."

If only it could have been that easy.

When I called Rad the next day and told him that Patricia was with me, he confirmed that he had assumed as much and had, in fact, convinced the Vargas men that it was better this way. They all knew that Patricia had let Rachel's disappearance affect her, maybe more than it should have, and Rad reassured Oscar Vargas that I could be trusted, that I might even calm her down, although I had not made much of an impression at the hotel bar.

"Oscar, Jaime, and me are staying at the hotel for another couple of days. I'm going to go over, again, everything I've got my hands on about Rachel since I was hired. Kodiack is on a book tour for his new novel. He's supposed to be in Denver in two days, so we might as well wait and talk to him again. He isn't going to like it, but I'd rather have him mad at me than old man Vargas."

"You're right about that. I think all those old Spanish gold coins that Vargas must have laying around the castle can buy a lot more heat than a few royalty checks from a writer who gets good reviews but not many sales. At least that's what I read in the book section of *People* magazine."

Rad laughed. "Louie, no matter what anybody else says, I think you're all right. Seriously, thanks for dealing with Patricia. You'll keep her out of our hair, and, between you and me, the three Vargases don't mix well when they're forced to act like a family. Just keep a close eye on her. She has, uh, problems, you know?"

"No shit, Rad. I thought she was just another sweet young debutante with bad table manners."

"Be careful with her, Louie. She's a high-maintenance young lady—unstable and prone to overreaction. If she loses it or gets hurt, Vargas will hold you responsible, even though I know it won't be your fault. She's already halfway in a straitjacket. You ask me, I think you bit off more than you should have. Patricia is out there, Louie, out there."

I hung up and thought over what Rad had said. Out there. Now that was a family trait that probably wasn't listed in the Southern California Blue Blood Directory. Out there. That had been exactly the way my old pal Coangelo had described Rachel. Out there.

But where? I had to ask. Where in the hell was she?

15

◆

From my father's backyard I stared at the distant haze hugging the front range. Looking west from Denver's Westside, I could see the edge of the city against the background of Colorado's famous peaks. A pale afternoon moon floated above the Rocky Mountains in a clear, powder blue sky. Distinct and obvious, it mocked the murkiness of the relationships that had been thrust on me since Rachel Espinoza/Vargas had brashly introduced herself.

The mountains kept their distance from the nastiness of the city, and although I had never been much of a nature lover, I could not shake the sensation that I had lost something—missed out on something—by growing up in the hustle and noise of Denver, oblivious to the splendor of the craggy peaks and deep woods.

Not that I believed I had been deprived. On the contrary, I knew that I had to live in the city. What I felt for my hometown may not have been love, but it came close.

I had my own memories and reference points, my own construct of what mattered and why, and that came from my life in the city, as a child and as an adult, and no matter what they might mean to anyone else, for me they would do and that had been sufficient. My pulse had the beat and rhythm of the streets, something different from the laid-back silence of the country, and assuredly it was not simple regret that caused me to dwell on what could have been if my father had decided to raise his family in one of the small towns that made up most of the rest of the state.

A group of boys played in the street next to my father's yard, and I recognized the tests of adolescence that easily evolved into spontaneous reckless games of dodging traffic. Customized minibikes mixed with young boxers who wore their baseball caps backwards. The rowdy bunch ended up in a junk-littered lot where they hollered and screamed at each other.

I knew from what Rad had told me that the Vargas children had nothing like those games for memories. They had been sheltered and protected from inevitable city temptations and unexpected rural challenges. They had grown up among the rolling hills and valleys of the land that had been preserved and protected by their family for hundreds of years. The words Rad used when he described Rancho Vargas made me think of an old English movie set on the gothic estate of a wealthy lord. The house had to be majestic but cold, maybe built on a cliff that overlooked the pounding ocean, and the land itself must have been beautiful but isolated and lonely. Rad had not described anything like that, but his tone of reverence—awe, actually—set it up in my head, and that was the image I carried whenever I thought about the Vargas children growing up on their father's hacienda.

Their entertainment had always been hired, bought and paid for so that the Vargas siblings had to do very little to create diversions from the clothes and toys that filled their rooms. From ponies at the family picnics to trips around the country club's golf course in electric carts, Jaime, Rachel, Patricia, and Francisco did not worry about things that my friends and I had accepted as normal.

I did not mean the omnipresent specter of hatred and violence that had shaped my cynical heart, and that had been born in cramped urban neighborhoods bursting with scrambling people all scrounging for a buck. The Vargas kids never had to deal with anything like that, of course, but then they had never experienced the exuberance of riding bicycles on the streets with ten wild children speeding through the night, the summer air whipping through their clothes, danger and freedom igniting the young minds that rejected the fact that they were late in getting home. Rachel and Patricia were never late getting home, until they rebelled to the point where they could ignore going home altogether and they simply stayed out all night.

I jiggled a loose board in the fence and a twisted nail fell from the rickety wood and bounced in the white rocks that Jesús had arranged around the beds of his rosebushes. I bet myself that Oscar and his wife had not deemed it necessary to warn Patricia about the hazards of lockjaw from stepping on a rusty nail—hell, by the time Patricia had finally seen a rusty nail she must have been associating with people who pierced various body parts with provocative pieces of metal, and tetanus had to have sounded like a harmless childhood disease.

I thought about leaving and checking in at my home/office. I was not ready for another night twisting and turning on the loose springs in my Dad's couch, and Jesús and Patricia had adapted to each other quite well. I could leave and not have to feel any twinge of conscience about how my lifestyle contortions had dumped a bundle of high-strung human emotional wreckage in my father's living room. And I wasn't referring to myself.

The taxi eased around the corner and slowly passed in front of me. It rolled to the curb and parked. Oscar Vargas emerged from the backseat. He stood as if in slow motion and stretched before he turned in my direction. He gave me a limp-wristed wave and trudged to the waist-high pickets that usually kept the riffraff off my father's impeccable backyard lawn. The cab drove away.

"Mr. Montez. I'm happy I found you here. Conrad told me where you had taken Patricia. And I thought . . . that is, that I should see for myself how she is doing. It's very convenient that you are here, too. We haven't had the chance to have a good talk about all this."

He stretched his arm in a dramatic gesture that took in all the area south of Colfax bordered by Santa Fe and Federal Boulevards, but he did not want to talk about the state of Westside politics or the annual Westside Clean-Up! campaign, or anything about the Westside, for that matter.

"Patricia's still asleep. My father says she had a rough night. Your youngest daughter is not well, Mr. Vargas. In more ways than one."

He cleared his throat and leaned against the fence. Something always seemed to be stuck deep inside his esophagus.

"Yes, of course, I am aware of her problems. Maybe not all of them, but a father knows more than his children ever suspect."

The grandness I had encountered in the hotel bar wavered. His hands shook, slightly, and the daylight highlighted the imperfections brought on by age.

He asked, "Are you a father, Mr. Montez?"

I did not appreciate the question. I believed that it was not any of his business, and his tone reminded me that certain people believe they are entitled to know or ask about anything they want, simply because of who they are. Like lawyers, for example. On the other hand, it could have been a harmless question—a question that probably was completely innocent, the type of question that people normally ask other people, a point of human interest. I concluded that my reaction was unreasonable, just another ragged part of the Louie Montez character that had to be smoothed out. So I went along, but I did not feel easy with it.

"I have two sons. They live with their mother. The oldest is away at a baseball camp. He hopes to make the varsity team, so he spends extra time working on his game. Good glove, quick feet, strong arm, no bat. Typical Latino shortstop."

Vargas nodded as though he understood my blubbering.

"The youngest may pop up around here. He visits his grandfather on a pretty regular basis. They have a good relationship."

I paused, hoping he would take my handoff and run with it. But he only nodded again.

I said, "To tell you the truth, I'm not the world's greatest father."

I could see the words, the ones I wanted to use, but they went unsaid. *"But I must be better than you, because my kids are nowhere near as screwed up as the heirs to the Vargas fortune seem to be, at least the female ones."*

Oscar Vargas finally responded. "I've never met a man

who thought he was. A good father, I mean. Being a father is one of those things that can never be done as well as it should. And for some of us, we never even get close."

He turned and looked at the view I had been admiring only a few minutes before. Neither one of us said anything for a few minutes. The noisy crowd of boys had moved from the lot into the yard of one of the neighbors, where they formed a huddle and spoke in exaggerated hushed whispers.

"Tell me, please, Montez, if you know. Or if you find out. Tell me what it is that Patricia is hurting about. If it's me, or something I've done, then I think I should hear it, and I think I can do something about it. But this not knowing, this silence and separation that she has thrown in all of our faces—that's what I can't take. I'm telling you because you've talked with her, and she's trusted you to let you try to take care of her. That's more than she's let me do for a long time. If you know what she will accept from me, please tell me. I do have a right."

"Somehow, I don't think anybody's rights are going to make a difference. Sometimes you take care of a person even when they say you can't. But—what can I say to you that will matter? She's in pain about Rachel, but that's not all of it. At least I don't think so. How long has this been going on?"

Vargas said, "Patricia has always been the delicate one, the one who was always sick, the one who would get lost in the park, the one bitten by a wasp, or chased by a dog. When her mother died, it . . . made it even worse, naturally. I did what I could, but . . . she needed extra attention, and I couldn't give it. Rachel was her closest friend, not just her sister, and Patricia had to lean on her for strength. Rachel's disappearance has . . ."

He did not try to finish.

"You may not like this question, but could Patricia have wanted Rachel to be out of the way? Jealousy or rivalry or anything like that?"

He shook his head vigorously. "No, no, Mr. Montez. As I said, Patricia is even more lost without Rachel. There is nothing she could have gained from Rachel leaving, except more loneliness. Patricia may be weak and dependent, but she is not someone who would hurt the only real friend she had."

"Patricia may have loved Rachel, but she also thought that Rachel's spot in the family had come about only because of a fortuitous accident. What would Patricia do if she resented Rachel, if she thought the intruder was getting all the attention, all the love that she thought she deserved?"

His eyes clearly expressed his feelings. He had asked for my input, but he could not have been expecting what he must have thought was impudence.

"Mr. Montez, even if Patricia could think of something so warped, she doesn't have the strength to do it. She's not the strong one in the family. Rachel's adoption has nothing to do with any of this!"

Another cab pulled up in front of my father's suddenly popular residence. Jaime Vargas climbed out of this one in almost the identical manner that his father had used only a few minutes before, except that his wave was heartier and his walk to the fence much more vigorous.

"Dad, I wish you had told me where you were going before you left the hotel. I was worried. Thank God Conrad knew what you planned to do. We don't need another one in the family to vanish."

He smiled, and I thought that maybe he did not mean to be as accusatory as his words had sounded. But the smile did not last and the cursory nod he gave me indicated that I had something to do with his father's apparently impetuous behavior.

Oscar said, "Jaime, quit worrying about me! Your sisters are the ones that we have to take care of—both of them. I came out here to talk with Mr. Montez, and with Patricia if she will see me."

The son grabbed his father around his shoulders. "Dad, I know you're only concerned about Rachel. I was worried about you, and her, that's all. We have to work together on this. Now, what have you and Mr. Montez decided to do?"

Before he said anything in response Patricia appeared at the back door.

The steadiness of her voice surprised me. "Dad. Come in. I'm sorry about last night. Come in and we can talk."

A look of triumph filled his face and he marched to his daughter without saying another word to Jaime or me. When Oscar finished hugging his youngest daughter and had slipped into the house, Jaime turned his attention to me.

"I know you are a good man, Montez. But please, remember that my father is old, not the man he used to be. He's sentimental and emotional, and his memory is half gone some days. I worry that he can be easily manipulated, you know? Not that that's what you were doing, don't get me wrong. I truly believe, at least, I think Rachel will turn up of her own accord, and this search nonsense is just to appease my father. But he's so upset that I'm afraid his judgment has been affected."

"Sure, I think I understand."

I tried to sound polite but I did not have any luck suppressing the rancor that hung bitterly at the edge of my throat. I had met everybody in the family except the youngest son, Francisco, and so far I hadn't really cot-

142

toned up to any one of them except during my brief fantasy about Rachel and the beach.

Conrad had filled me in on some of Jaime's background. The Vargas family had interests in enterprises that struck me as blatantly Californian—high-tech gadgets for business computers, trendy restaurants, and a growing chain-store empire strung up and down the coast that catered to the health-conscious elite. Village Vargas, Ltd., offered power candy bars, vitamins and no-fat tortilla chips, the latest exercise machines, and ancient cures and remedies advertised as adapted from authentic Native American traditions.

Jaime Vargas had his fingers in all of those pies. With his family name and his Stanford MBA, he provided the punch and authority for the business decisions on which Oscar Vargas had gradually spent less and less time.

Conrad had told me: "Jaime walked in right where his father had stood all those years, and the transition didn't cause more than a ripple in the financial weeklies. From what I hear, he's good at what he does. Probably a better businessman than his father. Devoted to his father, he hasn't married, yet, but he's one of the state's more eligible bachelors. Politics seems like a good bet for him, one day. Hispanic, rich, business leader. A good governor candidate for either party, when he finally decides to do it."

Jaime Vargas, potential future governor of the great state of California, let out a deep breath and looked around the neighborhood, trying his damnedest to find something that we could talk about. When he realized there was not much to grab his attention except aging houses and one-way traffic, he quit trying.

"Rachel always was a devil, the wild one who pushed us to our limits. We could count on her to provide excitement, even when we didn't want any."

"I think this is more than a prank," I responded, "She's disappeared, and no one has even tried to contact the family. I don't want to unduly worry you, but it could be worse than your father is willing to accept right now."

"So true. We shall see. Dad can be tough when he has to, even though he gets a bit distracted."

There did not seem to be anything else to talk about. It all sounded so final.

"Tell me, Montez, what do you do for relaxation? I know you're a lawyer and Conrad told us about a few cases you've worked on in the past, and some of the rather interesting sidelines your cases have taken you to. But what about after hours, for fun?"

The question caught me off guard. Not only was it unexpected, but it struck me as inappropriate, given the circumstances.

"I listen to music, catch a baseball game when I can, drink too much beer and sometimes too much Canadian whiskey. I go for long walks in the interest of my botched-up knee, and once in a while I spend time with my father or my sons. But that's not what you mean, is it?"

"Heh-heh. No, Montez, it's not. I mean real fun. How about women, or gambling? I don't mean to pry, but I guess I'm asking for my own sake. I don't like baseball, I rarely drink beer or whiskey, I have no children, and right now my father is occupied with his daughters. You see what I mean?"

I thought that I had just seen another reason why Jaime Vargas had not launched his political career. He had not yet finished creating the skeletons in his closet that one day were sure to be exposed, and he would have to deal with the scandal that most elected officials took for granted in the years since Nixon ungracefully jumped from the White House and Teddy Kennedy hastily jumped out of the car sinking under the bridge.

I have had clients ask me the same kind of question. A guy who knew he was on his way to prison wanted me to arrange a party for him, as he called it. I reminded him that my retainer did not include social events that required me to pimp, and he quickly dropped the idea. In bars, when it's late and fuzzy, sometimes someone will start talking about finding "a woman" or "a game." The few times I have gone down either one of those roads I have regretted it, usually because the guy whose idea it was passed out before the action really started and I had to talk my way out of something that I did not belong in, or understand. Now the same question was being asked of me, in broad daylight, from a man who had more money invested in his haircut than I had in my checking account, and alcohol or potential incarceration had nothing to do with it.

"I can't help you, Jaime. I'm sure there's someone at the hotel who knows more about where to look for what you need than I do. We better go in and see how everyone's doing."

I turned and walked away, quickly.

I had been in the house for several minutes, assisting my father with a snack for Oscar and Patricia, when Jaime finally entered. He introduced himself to Jesús, sat at the table, and quietly drank a glass of iced tea. They were replaying a routine they had performed many times before, all three of them. Father and daughter absolved each other of all grievances that had reopened the rift between them, while Jaime patiently waited until the scene played itself out and he could reassert himself as the real head of the family.

After Oscar and Jaime left, and Patricia had promised

to return to the hotel "in the next day or two," it was time for me to leave. Patricia bussed me on the cheek, then curled up in front of Dad's TV.

Jesús escorted me out of his house and his only comment was, "*¿Por qué no hablaron de Rachel?* Why was there no talk about the missing girl? What kind of people are they, Louie?"

My father always asked the right questions. If only he were as good with the answers.

16

My career as a lawyer had ground to a serious slow-down since the unfortunate Wilson Lopez had gone to extreme measures to avoid paying my bill. A few case files lay exposed on my desk, and I had a couple of messages from potential clients on my answering machine, but nothing that made me want to pay up my very late dues to the Hispanic Bar Association. I no longer received the association's newsletter, and that gave me a bit of a pause because I knew of lawyers who still were on the association's mailing list although they had died years ago. Reestablishing myself as the fine, super fine legal eagle I knew I had been, and could be again, had turned out to be tougher than I had anticipated, even in my most negative period when I had stared at the hospital ceiling waiting for my knee to quit draining whatever it was that the nurses gingerly carted away in plastic bags, gloom and doom written all over their pretty faces.

I worked on the few cases for an hour or so, until I

faced up to the truth that I couldn't milk many more bill-
able hours out of trying to create a defense for clients like
Steve Mesa. He owed the state the welfare that had been
paid for his kid when he had "forgotten" to make his
child-support payments, and it really did not matter that
his ex-wife had prevented him from seeing the kid for several months. If Luis Montez was not won over to the concept that Steve had tried all that hard to keep up with his
visitation—his parenting time as the family court judges
liked to call it—then there was no way that a social services "technician" was going to buy into any of my ratio-
nalizations. Besides, as I told my male clients more times
than I kept track of anymore, parenting time and child
support had very little to do with each other, no matter
what a slick cousin said he had used to get out from
under the child-support hammer.

A short taste of iced Canadian and a few pages of *The
Autobiography of a Brown Buffalo* moved me in a direction I had avoided since I had overindulged on a killer
lunch with Rodney. The bond between Bobby Baca and
Chick Montero had nagged at me like an infected insect
bite, but with the Vargases in town I had not had the time
to scratch it.

I called the poet to set up a meeting.

Without any preliminary small talk, I asked Bobby
Baca if he would talk with me. Before I could explain what
about, he insisted that I meet him at the Globeville Rec
Center. His impatience was fueled by an agitation whose
source I did not know and he did not think I had to understand.

"Tonight, Louie. At the rec center, around ten. I'll be
there with a group of students who are working with me
on Charlotte's book. It's way out of hand. I need a break
from this mess."

Rad and I sat in a corner of the public library surrounded by windows and bookshelves. The gleam from his earring bounced wildly and occasionally glinted into my range of vision, causing me to squint. Summer had returned after one night of reluctant cooling down, and with it came the harsh, straight-edged sunshine that bears down on Coloradans and produces abnormal skin-cancer statistics.

The second-floor alcove was hot and stuffy, but it was where Rad had gone to think about his case, and where he had wanted to meet me for our long overdue conversation. After my quick talk with Baca, Rad had called. Rather than try to get everything out over the phone, I had suggested a face-to-face. He agreed and then I consented to meet him at the downtown library where he was doing some research.

The venerable building at Broadway and Fourteenth Avenue was scheduled for a facelift, and I already missed the easy access to information that the place had provided over the years. The new library had to be bigger and, therefore, more difficult to use, even though it might be better looking. But Denver was changing—new airport and baseball stadium, light rail, and, next, the library—new and prettier accoutrements for the queen of the plains, and there was not much I could do about the accessorization of my hometown. There were days when I did not recognize the city. I was amazed at what the city planners had accomplished—a light rail system that did not go anywhere (unless you were one of the few looking for lunch at Hot Rodney's), a new airport that, so far, had no planes, and, because of the baseball strike, a new sports team without players.

I quit worrying about matters of civic pride and returned to the more immediate issue of how I was going to deal with Rad Valdez.

My agenda included the bit from Concep and my doubts about Rad's seemingly innocent role in the fire. Rad made it clear that he wanted to press me for details about the missing manuscript, and more about what Rachel and I had talked about in Mexico. Despite his reassurances to Oscar Vargas, he obviously was not all that convinced that I was not keeping something to myself about the book.

A pair of homeless men slept with their heads buried in their arms on the desk in the corner, and even from several yards away I could tell that they had not taken recent advantage of the shower at the shelter. A kinetic, buzzing group of students in shorts and T-shirts sprawled across a table and several chairs near the windows. They looked harried and desperate, and whatever they were working on must have been due any minute.

Spread out on the table where Rad sat were collections of poetry that included Charlotte Garcia and Bobby Baca, copies of old magazine articles about Oscar Acosta, a newspaper story about Brian Gulf's last big movie, and several reviews of Mel Kodiack's most recent book.

I picked up a thin volume. The lettering along the spine read LOS ANGELES ON THE EDGE. It was an overview of the young, avant-garde Los Angeles art community. Rad had marked a page that briefly described the work of Isela Vega, Rachel's performance artist friend. I read:

> Vega brings to her work the awareness of a
> brash Latina, raised in the suburbs of Los An-
> geles, who turned her back on her middle-class
> upbringing only to outrage audiences from every
> class. With lurid and what some call vulgar im-

ages flickering in the background, Vega rotates between beating a Native American drum, playing a South American flute, and shaking a North American cowbell while she sings, hollers, cries, and silently mouths her message of high-tech depression, religious hypocrisy, and male-bashing epithets. She is not an easy artist to watch.

I offered my view to Rad. "That kind of review should have sent Vega into spasms of appreciation. She must have loved it. 'Not an easy artist to watch.' What more could someone on the edge ask for?"

"I saw her act. Once. I had to leave before it finished. When she brought an old whiskered billy goat on stage that had only three legs, and started whipping a butcher knife through the air, I figured I had gotten the point, and if I hadn't, I didn't really need it. Rachel never let me forget that I walked out before I saw the entire performance. Needless to say, Rachel was a big fan."

"Vega was in Mexico, right? I never saw her. Did Kodiack?"

"No. He said that Vega was gone when he arrived. I can't quite put the time line together. Rachel, Vega, Gulf, and Kodiack are all in Mexico in the same week, in the same condo, but it doesn't look as though they were really together."

"And so far we can't ask Rachel about it. How about this artist?"

He shook his head.

"Nothing. She's never been, uh, approachable, in the normal sense. Can't get a line on her."

I returned the book to Rad's pile of research materials. No more beating around the bush. No more questions whose answers I already knew. It was time for me to deal with the doubts that Concepción Sanchez had planted.

"You know, Rad, I almost feel that way about you. Can't quite get a line on you, figure you out. I thought I understood where you're coming from. Young guy, shaky about his heritage, but tough and trying to do his job."

"So far, you got it right."

He leaned back in his chair and waited to see where I was going with all the personal stuff.

"I saw something in you that I admired."

"And you don't anymore? What is this, Louie?"

"I don't know, for sure. Nagging doubt, that's it."

His smile grew even broader and I could see that he wanted me to talk about whatever it was that was bugging me. He wanted to get it out and over.

"*Tu eres mi otro yo.* You are my other self. I see myself in you, Rad, so many years ago, and yet—"

"I don't have a clue about where you're going with this. I hope it has something to do with Rachel, or Charlotte at least."

I grabbed a chair and straddled its back—a symbolic barrier between the West Coast PI and the Colorado attorney, who both had something in common that transcended geography or profession but who were having a hell of a time figuring out just what that was.

"Okay, tell me this. Concep Sanchez said that the 'Hole fire had something to do with a guy from California. A warning to back off whatever it was that the guy was into. That sounds like you, Rad. But you have been telling me the same story over and over. You had no idea about the fire. No insight, no other leads on it, except what it looks like—a careless bit of arson that went too far. But Sanchez, whose word I trust in certain matters, painted a pretty good picture of you. Too coincidental to be anyone else. That leads me to only one place. Who's trying to make you back off, Rad? Who lit up the 'Hole as a warning to you? Who killed Charlotte, by mistake, because they were trying to get to you?"

His smile stayed, but he sat upright in his chair and clenched his hands on the hard wood of the table.

"I got to hand it to you, Louie. You got more out of Sanchez than I did. He wouldn't open up for anything—money, threats, nothing. Thought I was just another cop. I knew he would talk with you. Of course, he had to know something that would get you hot under the collar. That kid knows everything that goes on in Globeville, even though it ain't much. I've seen his type all over the run-down neighborhoods of L.A., from East Los Angeles to Compton. Street punks who know the score but can't figure out how to find a job."

"Right. I know all about alienated youth. That's not the point. Who is it, Rad? There are only two possibilities, the way I see it. You are the target, or you are the guy who set it up. Either way, your silence probably cost Charlotte her life."

The smile vanished.

"Don't lay that on me. I didn't have anything to do with the fire. I'm not an arsonist, a killer. I'm a PI doing my job, and sometimes that means that I get in people's faces, step on toes, and make myself unwelcome. I don't give a shit, Louie. If there was anything I could have done to save Charlotte, I would have. There wasn't."

He paused, looked around the room, studied the faces of some of the library's customers, then returned to me.

I leaned harder against the chair back. I wasn't going anywhere, and I had all the time in the world. If he lashed out at me with his well-trained feet and rock-hard hands, I did not have a chance. If he talked to me, told me the truth, our relationship would be changed forever, one way or the other.

How well did I know Conrad Valdez? If he was a killer, then nothing, or nobody, would stop him from quickly but efficiently smashing my head into pulp, running out of the library, and disappearing into the afternoon crowd of tourists and shoppers. I hoped that he wasn't a killer.

Once again, he gave the second floor of the library the once-over. He was more nervous than I had ever seen him.

"I've been getting warnings ever since I got hired by old man Vargas. Someone does not want me nosing around about Rachel. These things happen. I don't go around telling everyone I meet about the perils of my occupation. It's there, that's all. I never took the warnings seriously, but they made me more concerned about Rachel. Something is going on with her that has somebody very uptight about my investigation. For all I know, the warnings could have come from you, Louie. You were one of the last people to see Rachel. You were attracted to her. That's been obvious since I first talked to you about her. Maybe you got carried away in Mexico. Maybe one of Rachel's trips went too far and you couldn't handle it, and she's dead. You don't want me to find that out so you tried to scare me off. The torching of the Keyhole might have been your way of getting me off your ass."

He had opened up and I breathed easier. He wanted to talk, even though he was saying crazy things, and that meant that I did not have to worry about my knee getting reinjured when I tried to jump out of his way. For a few minutes, at least, catching one of his nice-looking size tens with my temple was not an option.

"You were warned to back off, to stay out of Denver, or what? What kind of warnings?"

"Phone calls, letters, notes pushed under my hotel door. Before I got together with you the night of the fire, I got a card that said things were going to get a lot hotter for me if I didn't tell old man Vargas that I was quitting. But I didn't know that meant that there was going to be a fire at the Keyhole. How could I? I didn't even know where you were taking me that night. You see how I could think that you were the one who was trying to keep me out of this case. You knew where we were going, you knew what kind of place it was, you knew where you had to be when the firebomb was thrown so that you could get out. And you're the person who had Rachel's manuscript and lost it."

It sounded so good that I started to wonder about myself. I was getting confused, so I tried to steer him back to the point, my point.

"You don't really believe that, or you would have kept me out of this altogether. You know I'm not your guy. You said you've been getting warnings since you started this case. I wasn't around then. I didn't know you, you didn't know me. Have there been other close calls like the fire?"

"I thought that holdup was part of it, but it doesn't look like it now. The Torres brothers were just a touch of local color that I stumbled on in your friendly hometown. But . . ."

"But what? What else?"

"In Montana, someone shot at me as I drove to Kodiack's cabin. It was a warning shot, I'm sure. One slug tore up the fender of my car. I stopped and got out of the car. Stupid, but I didn't know what had happened until I saw the bullet hole. Then I dived for cover, before I realized that the shooter had had several seconds when he could have plugged me, and he hadn't, so it had to be another warning. I don't think the guy wants to kill me, just scare me off. At least so far. And remember, Louie, you knew I was going to Montana."

"You could be telling me the truth, or you could be making this all up. How would I ever know? Maybe it's you who has something to hide. Maybe you're the one who finally had your fill of Rachel's lifestyle, after she led you around for a couple of years, while she partied with whoever she wanted, took off for Mexico without you whenever she wanted. Had her special friends like Mel Kodiack and this weirdo Vega. Maybe you realized you didn't fit in with Rachel and you couldn't take it. You see, Rad, neither one of us is so clearly innocent, and yet neither one of us can afford to not trust the other."

My scenario had affected him. His usually glistening eyes dimmed and small, sharp wrinkles tugged at the corners of eyelids. What I said was too close to the truth, but, I hoped, not all of it.

I said, "I think we have what John Wayne used to call a Mexican stand-off. Now what?"

"It's your move, Louie. I told you my doubts, but I also am going to play this out until I find Rachel. I've worked with you so far, I guess I go on that way until I have to stop because I find out the truth, about you if necessary, or one of us gets killed."

I thought that was a bit more than I was willing to contribute to the cause.

"You said you got a card the night of the fire. What was that? What was on it?"

He reached into his vest pocket and handed me a piece of cardboard about the size of a wedding announcement. The words stared at me in black ink and block letters.

GO BACK TO CALIFORNIA. THE HEAT IS ONLY STARTING.
QUIT FUCKING AROUND AND PACK UP AND GET OUT.
YOU WON'T LIKE WHAT YOU MIGHT FIND.
I'LL KILL YOU IF I HAVE TO.

I spent about an hour in the library with Rad. We said only a few more words to each other, then I did my own research. I found a book, apparently written by a graduate student, about the pioneers of California, and, in Chapter 8, I read about the Vargas family from the 1600s to the present. There was more color in the early part of the history—assorted religious zealots, highway bandits, and smugglers—typical western frontier highjinks, but there was more detail about the generation that included Oscar Vargas and his offspring. Even in the objective narrative of someone's doctoral thesis, it was clear that the patriarch had sown a few seeds that had strayed far from the family's grape arbors. Jaime appeared to have more in common with his old man than I had originally thought.

We said an uneasy good-bye, each one of us anticipating that we would come up with a show of unity before the interview with Kodiack. We still worked together, in the informal way we had since we had bumped into each other in Tapia's store, but now we had something new in the mix. It remained to be seen how far that would take us.

Jesús looked surprised when he opened his door and saw my face. Unannounced visits from me were rare.

"Must be that Vargas girl again. You missed her. She's back at the hotel with her father. Haven't seen you twice in one week since you quit borrowing money from me. Seen more of Patricia lately. What you need, Luis?"

"I visit all the time. Don't start. Actually, it is business but I'm not looking for Patricia. That package that I left here. I need it. Time to read it again."

He shuffled off to his bedroom and in a few minutes he returned, carrying the worn box in which Rachel had presented her book. I was on the phone as he placed the box on the kitchen table. He returned to his tiny garden in the back corner of his yard. I removed the ribbon and lifted Rachel's manuscript at the same time that Rodney Harrison agreed to do some late-night second-chairing.

"Okay, I'll be at the Globeville Rec Center around ten. I'll have to meet you there, I got to close up. So I just stay in the shadows, so to speak, watch your back. Let you know if I see Chick Montero anywhere around the joint. Sounds crazy, but you're the man, Louie. Later."

A quiet hour and a half passed. Jesús interrupted me with an offer of a glass of iced tea. He asked, "When are you going to show that to the investigator? He still thinks it's stolen, doesn't he? *¿Qué pasa?*"

"I have to read it closely, see what the hell was going on with Rachel. This investigator—I don't know, Dad. Things have changed. Maybe after this weekend, after I hear from the writer Kodiack myself. Maybe then I'll give this to Valdez."

"Whatever, Luis. You always have had a strange way of doing things. Ha! A strange life, what am I saying?"

He muttered some more, and puttered around the room for a few minutes, and then I lost track of him. I had come to the part of Rachel's book where the ten-year-old daughter starts talking about the night she saw her father killed. There were some good passages about the girl's terror and fright, and then her resourcefulness as she hid herself from the killer. It flowed and I was caught up in the suspense. I actually worried about the young girl trapped by the unknown killer who had already showed the magnitude of his horror by brutally dispatching her father.

There was only one thing. A short passage that seemed out of context, that did not quite fit with the overall story line, with the general mood of Rachel's attempt at a mystery novel:

She wanted to cry, but she kept it in. It was not the time or place for tears. Those would come later, when it was right, when she saw him again and told him it was over, and she would end his life as easily as he had ruined hers.

What the hell?

17

Weeds Lopez haunted me. No other way to say it. His death in my front yard represented a really bad loose end. He had hired me to straighten out his troubles with Albert Kopinski, and all I had offered him was the likelihood that a judge would lecture his antagonist. That's what lawyers do, I kept telling myself. I should not feel beat about the way things turned out. He had been involved with guys like Kopinski, a man with whom I had never had a pleasant experience, and Montero, whom I knew only by reputation, which was not good. Weeds must have appreciated the odds on how those kinds of relationships end. And, *ya sabes,* I did not even like the guy, especially after I heard his whining recital of the story about the money that Kopinski had fronted to save his hide. Weeds Lopez haunted me.

Meeting Baca seemed the only way to get rid of that particular demon. Baca's association with Montero had jolted me when I had learned about it, and then on top of that there was the link between Montero and Kopin-ski. As much as I hated what I was doing, I thought I had no choice. I would confront Baca, get to the bottom of his dealings with Montero, and try to put it together. Did Baca have anything to do with the killing of Wilson Lopez?

My knee throbbed and I rubbed it methodically as I drove to Globeville. North on I-25, east on I-70 to the Brighton Boulevard exit, and then around a few blocks until I arrived at the building where I was to meet the poet. The knee pained me all the way.

Two cars sat in the lot, a beat-up van and a late-model sedan. I recognized the van as Bobby's. As I walked by the sedan, rap music blared into the night. A sullen young man sat in the driver's seat, smoking a cigarette and generally looking as though he had better things to do.

Sal Castro was away with the center's baseball team at a tournament in Pueblo and so that meant that the center was, for all practical purposes, closed. No one on the small staff stayed during the night unless they had a special project going on with the kids. That night, it had been only Baca and his crew, and a sculpture class that had finished hours before.

Baca worked with a group of kids who met at the center every week to talk about writing—poetry—and, since the fire, to put together the memorial for Charlotte. He should have been finished by the time I showed up, and when I walked into the gray, nondescript, and sterile building where teens were supposed to find an alternative to the excitement of the street, the place was very near to empty.

He was using a corner room with a rectangular table where the cutting and pasting took place. He hunched over the pages of the proposed book, and next to him was an ungainly young girl who moved pieces of text and illustrations so that they could study the overall effect. A computer sat on the floor, unused, although it must have offered a quicker method for designing the mock-up. Baca's weather-beaten portfolio lay next to the computer, also ignored.

They both looked up when I entered the room. Baca said, "Be right with you, Louie. Just a sec."

I gave my knee a break and braced myself against the cool concrete wall. Baca finished what they had been working on and told the girl that she had kept her brother waiting too long in the parking lot.

"Catch your ride before he takes off on you."

She left and then Baca and I were the only persons in the building.

He said, "Nice to see you again. I need something for this thing for Charlotte. Like I told you before, with the intro. Since you won't do it, I need to find someone else. Any ideas?"

Although he asked, he didn't wait for an answer. He was busy closing up the building. He walked as he talked, and I followed him. He turned off light switches in the various rooms and checked locked doors. I shoved gym equipment into a storage locker. He emptied trash cans into a Dumpster next to the back door, piled lipstick-smudged cups in a sink, and hung a discarded sweater on a coat hook. He turned off lights everywhere he went. In a short time, we were in darkness except for the illumination from the light that stayed on in the lobby trophy case. Baca lit a cigarette and leaned against the wall.

"You've been asking around about me, Louie. You need to know anything, you should come to me, man. What gives?"

He was a shadow in the hallway, a few feet from me,

but I could not make out many details except when the cigarette glowed and his face came into focus.

"You must appreciate how it is, Bobby. Somehow, I'm involved with a couple of things that don't figure for me, things that I didn't think had any connection. But then, one day, there was a connection, a coincidence that I couldn't ignore, one of those things that come along and kick you in the pants and so you have to pay attention to it."

"What connection? What's it got to do with me? You're talking nonsense."

"You are the connection, Bobby. The fire and Charlotte's death. You were there. Weeds Lopez gets himself splattered on my street. Chick Montero, a guy that moves around the shadows of the Northside, was an associate of Weeds and, I learn, also was on your list of acquaintances. The fire, Weeds, Montero, and you. Coincidence? What do they add up to? That's why I been asking around about you, Bobby. I guess I don't really believe in coincidence."

He took a long pull on his cigarette, then dropped it on the floor and ground it out under his shoe.

"That's all bullshit. You're as screwy as they come if you think I had anything to do with running over Weeds Lopez. From what I hear, that was that Polack Kopinski. Get out of here, Montez, before I forget that we been friends for a long time. I might not overlook your bad manners."

He may have told me to leave, but he straddled the narrow hallway, blocking the path to the door. I remembered his legendary anger, his ferocious ranting and raving in public, but I had never heard of any private expressions of that rage. Almost everything about the man was legendary—poetry, oratory, campaigns for public office, "The Pachuco Song." Was I really accusing this legend of complicity in murder?

"I'll leave when I hear what I came to find out. How long it takes is up to you."

He moved in my direction but before he could grab me, something quivered in the soft light of the trophy case. A shadow crossed the front door. We froze. I looked at the trophy case and the front door, but nothing showed itself in the lobby. I dropped to the floor and tried to crawl into the seam along the concrete wall. Baca stayed on his feet. I was about to tell him to get down when I noticed the gun in his hand.

A voice echoed from the lobby all the way back to the empty bleachers of the gym.

"Baca! This is it! You're a dead man!"

Baca inched along the wall, gripping his gun with both hands, his head turning in both directions as he looked for the source of the voice.

He shouted into the darkness, "Montero! You ain't getting anything else from me! Fuck you, Montero!"

His words came out in a long, wailing scream. He rushed to the front door, stretching his gun straight in front of him as though that was all he needed to protect himself. Bullets shattered the glass. Baca screamed again. He fell forward.

I sprang to my knees and immediately regretted it. The twinge from my wounded knee slammed through me like a six-foot hypodermic. Baca made no other sounds. I waited for several seconds, then I gingerly crawled down the hall to the body. My hand felt something wet, sticky, and warm. Blood flowed along the floor. I stopped when I heard the footsteps on broken glass. I swept up Baca's gun from against the wall. It was bloody but I held it close and waited for Montero to show his face in the light of the doorway. I felt his presence before I saw him. A ray of light caromed into the hallway off the intruder's hand.

"Louie? Hey, Louie. You all right?"

I breathed again and dropped the gun.

"Rodney. Over here. Quick. We got to call the cops, and an ambulance."

He stepped into the hallway. His shiny razor rested in his tight fist, ready to carve anything that foolishly challenged its deadly bite.

"Fucking A . . . What happened?"

"I'm not sure I know, Rodney. Baca needs a doctor, something."

Rodney checked Baca for vital signs.

"If this guy was a poet, his verses are finished. Sorry, Louie, but your friend here's dead."

"I had to stay at the restaurant later than I expected. When I got here, I pulled into the lot and a car went tearing by me. No lights. I couldn't see the driver. Must have been the shooter."

I nodded, then I asked Rodney Harrison to stick out his neck again.

"The cops will be here soon, whether we call or not. I'm going to look through his stuff. Keep an eye out for the cops."

"What is it you expect to find?"

"Not sure. But only Baca and Montero know the truth, and since Baca ain't talking, and Montero didn't stick around to chat, the next best thing for me is if Baca had anything on him that might be useful. I'd like to get to his house, but the cops will be all over that as soon as they find out who he is. What do you say?"

"If the cops pull up, I'll holler, Louie. You only got a few minutes as it is."

I went through Baca's pockets but there was nothing except some loose change. I limped as quickly as I could to the room where he had worked with his students. A quick inventory gave me only his mock-up of Charlotte's book, pencils, pens, scissors and a glue stick, and his portfolio. I looked through it. Poems, mostly written in pencil, some that would never be finished, were secured by the thick cardboard covers of the case he had carried everywhere. Stuck between pages of a poem that obviously had been copied and recopied a number of times, I found a folded letter. I scanned the letter, untied my right shoelaces, folded the letter, and stuffed it into the bottom of my shoe.

I thought, That's even too stupid for you, Montez. I read the words again, then replaced it in the portfolio.

Rodney's whistle jerked me and I dropped the portfolio.

"Louie. They're here!"

I looked over the poems as they lay scattered on the floor. The fading, slightly askew typewritten stanzas that had hidden the letter were from Baca's epic: "Pachuco, Low Rider, Xicano." "The Pachuco Song." Baca's epitaph.

I told the police what I knew about Baca and my suspicions about Montero, but it was so incomplete that it could not have been all that persuasive. They said they would check into Montero, who no doubt had an alibi, but by the time they let Rodney and me leave the center, they had a different theory that solved the case.

"Another idiotic drive-by. This street's always getting shot up. Guy was in the wrong place at the wrong time."

Apparently killings in Globeville were more likely to be written off as unfortunate results of the neighborhood's general character than as the culmination of the bad mix between a small-time hood and a spotlight-seeking poet.

Charlotte's death also had been ascribed to the same "wrong place at the wrong time" supposition.

I did not argue. Baca had been murdered and it was no accident. But whether the police ever collared Chick Montero for the hit on Baca was not my concern. I had to come up with the remaining missing pieces—I still did not understand the Baca/Montero scenario, or whether it had anything to do with Charlotte Garcia. My urgent need to find out had nothing to do with bringing down the killer. Charlotte deserved to rest in peace, and her friend, Bonnie, had the right to know who killed her. Was Baca's entanglement with Montero somehow responsible for the fire? But I also was intent on learning what the truth was because of another friend, another contradiction in my special relationships. How did it fit in with Rad Valdez? Was I trying to implicate Baca so that I could be reassured about Rad, or was I on a trail that would end up with a truth that I really did not want to find? Whatever, I was on my way, and I was not sure how I was going to stop.

Under the steady light of my desk lamp, I reconstructed the paper I had retrieved from my shoe. Stealing it then returning it to its original hiding place had been a melodramatic and, as it turned out, unnecessary gesture. The police were just not that interested in either Rodney or me. The dead Bobby Baca, notorious cop-baiter and rabble-rouser, did not get much of a rise out of the police, and my appearance on the scene only reinforced their attitude that the shooting was just another incident involving off-kilter Mexicans. If they had had to break up a disturbance, spray Mace indiscriminately, and cleverly exercise their batons, then they would have had a strong impetus to make the extra effort. Since neither Rodney nor I gave them an opportunity to knock heads, they sent us home. They did promise to look us up again for another statement. Witnesses get interviewed numerous times by the police, but I didn't clear my calendar for their appearances at my office. I did not expect them to show.

The bitterness had never left me, even after years of trooping through the courtrooms and police buildings of the North American legal system where I had played the lawyer role for all it was worth. My father says I'm hopeless.

I stared at my legal pad and visualized the message that had spurred Baca into his desperate frame of mind. The short letter, more of a note, eloquently and simply conveyed the sentiment of the author, although Hallmark would never use it. Sloppy and erratic penmanship got right to the point.

> Baca—Your old pal Weeds has been taken care of. Your secret's safe—just between you and me. Guess what? Since that dumb ass song seems to be really important, I want what Weeds wanted, only double. Take care of it. Remember, I'm more careful than that stupid son of a bitch. And you already know what I can do if I have to.

No signature graced the message but if Chick Montero didn't write it, then Bobby Baca had died screaming the wrong name.

18

<small>◆</small>

Baca's death made sleep impossible until I had enough Canadian in me to calm the buzz left over from the shooting. An agony of disjointed fears, jaw-clenching anger, and pensive tossing and turning worked against any rest. The sweltering night finally brought on a darkness masquerading as sleep.

Sweat drenched my upper torso and the backs of my legs, and something wrapped around my waist so that I could not move. The woman whose voice whispered concern did not show her face. She created echoes of long-departed Evangelina, mysterious Teresa, and the ex-wives, but when I fixed on her, she sounded like no one I had ever met. Rachel's sensuality covered the night with a heavy perfume, a musk born of forbidden desire and illicit couplings.

"How do you get yourself into these situations? I don't know anybody like you, Louie. Don't you worry about what might happen to you?"

"I've been shot, beat up, run off the road, arrested, disbarred, and dumped by every woman who ever had the bad luck to trust me. My knee's ruined. What else can happen?"

"You could get killed. That seems to be the only thing left."

I knew I was dreaming but I did not want to wake up. I accepted the uneasy languor filled with quivering, effluvial images and baroque sounds. Only the woman's voice came through as precise, clear.

"Tu eres mi otro yo."

I gave Rad a ride to the book signing where we expected to meet Mel Kodiack. The Vargas men had driven on ahead. Patricia had excused herself from meeting the writer—"It will be a waste of time," she claimed, but I got the impression she wanted to avoid him.

Rad's energy level had increased with each mile closer to the bookstore. He had concluded that Kodiack held the key to finding Rachel.

"This guy may have made a name for himself with books about the wide-open West and the honorable, visionary men and women who settled the land, but he has his own dishonorable skeletons that I'm sure he doesn't want out."

"You found something on this guy?"

He nodded his head with the cocky assurance of young Chicanos that I had come to take for granted. It was either that or assume they all wanted to fight.

"Several wives, and the divorces were always messy. Domestic violence, restraining orders, police called in to keep the respective parties from seriously damaging each other. This was before he published his first book. Since then, he's stayed single, with several young women, if you know what I mean. No history of violence for a few years, but I did dig up a magazine interview with a starlet who claimed that she and Kodiack had lived together, done whopping amounts of drugs, thrown wild parties that sounded more like orgies, and generally trashed their friends and themselves. She said she left because he 'got out of hand,' whatever that means."

"What's that got to do with Rachel? He may not be a sensitive guy of the nineties, but so far you haven't tied Kodiack to Rachel's disappearance."

"The only thing I got, Louie, is that I know Rachel was infatuated with him—with his publicity image is more like it. She thought she was a writer. Kodiack really is a writer, a well-known one at that. He paid attention to her, encouraged her, I guess, and she fell for it. With his past instability, he had the potential to hurt Rachel. I don't want it to be that way, but it's something we have to consider."

"Sounds like Kodiack has more than his fair share of women. And now that he's famous, why risk everything over Rachel? What I read about Kodiack is that he seems to be on the verge of hitting it big. Book awards, a movie deal, honorary degrees. If anything can stop a man's violent tendencies, I would think that losing the potential for money and fame might do it. Don't you, Rad?"

He shrugged and went back to studying his notes.

Rad and Rachel made an odd couple. His attraction to her did not coincide with my view of him as a strait-laced, all-business young man with excessive drive and ambition, and her reputation as a high-flying hellion. But then I had never understood the combustible mix between men and women—my unbroken string of strike-outs attested to my inadequacies in the love department.

The investigator was too close to his subject, as I had

feared when I had first realized that he had a private stake in finding Rachel. His objectivity was gone, and with that went his usefulness in putting together the big picture. I hoped that we were not on a wild goose chase spurred on by Rad's jealousy. If I had been the one to get sucked into a dead end because I could not keep my heart and head separated, then that was one thing, and likely, anyway. But this time I was just the second banana along for the ride, the kemo sabe. Rad Valdez was the professional, and I was counting on him to lead the way.

Mel Kodiack knew how to create, and manipulate, an image. He dressed in what I called a safari jacket—khaki, past the waist, dozens of pockets, buckles and straps at every corner—and a broad-brimmed cloth hat bent over the eyebrows. Rugged outdoor shoes and badly faded denim jeans complemented the ruddiness of the patches of his face that glowed around his neat but bushy beard. His voice rolled over all other noises.

Rad, Jaime, Oscar, and I sat near the table where only a few minutes before he had been signing books for his readers, going to great lengths to amuse his customers with tales of the wild writer's life. The bookstore, one of the country's largest independents, had been busy with readers, buyers, and browsers when we arrived near the end of Kodiack's scheduled reading.

When the last Kodiack fan had been accommodated, the store quickly closed and the dawdlers were ushered out. We remained on Kodiack's okay. He had agreed to talk with us. We were surrounded by walls of books divided into various categories. The three-story store had thousands of books tucked into every nook and cranny, and mounds more had accumulated on most of the available floor space. I had a difficult time placing the tragedy of the vanished Rachel in the profoundly literate setting where I found myself with two of the wealthiest men in the state of California, an eager, ambitious private investigator, and an author about to break into the big time. Luis Montez, where will you end up next?

The woman who had arranged Kodiack's appearance excused herself by saying that she had some paperwork, and she disappeared into a small back office. We were to holler when we were ready to be let out of the store.

He quickly introduced himself to me, then turned to the subject at hand. He was not a man to waste time on small talk.

"Valdez, I know you all are rightly concerned about Rachel. But, honestly, I believe she is okay." Mel Kodiack cast his bright blue eyes on the old man. "Mr. Vargas, I can understand what you're going through. I lost a child a few years back. Leukemia. I wouldn't wish the agony of losing a daughter on anyone. It must be a nightmare. But Rachel is a strong person, one of the strongest women I ever met. She also is very independent. Hell! What am I saying? You all know that a hell of a lot better than I do!"

Oscar Vargas nodded. Jaime, who had been sitting quietly next to his father, spoke. "Mr. Kodiack. What was it that Rachel was planning to do? Where was she going when she left Mexico?"

"Well, she wasn't real explicit. Rachel told me she had a meeting set with this guy who claimed to be her, uh, her natural father. She was upbeat, excited. But no details. She didn't offer any, and I didn't pry. This Acosta thing is strange, I got to admit that. I doubt there is such a guy. If it wasn't just her character from the screenplay that she was submerging herself into, then sure she was planning to meet someone. But who knows for sure? It was hard for me to always tell where she was coming from."

Oscar Vargas frowned and looked very disturbed. Kodiack tried to salvage some optimism.

"Hey, she's probably off somewhere with this person, and she's neglected to let you know where she is. That's all. Rachel's done that kind of thing before. The first time she came down to Mexico, I remember, you all didn't know where she was. Remember? She told me about that, later. It's the same thing now. She'll turn up. I honestly think that."

I lifted one of his books from the table. The cover was a bold, unequivocal painting of a burly, bearded frontiersman, dressed in animal skins, standing in the bright sunshine of a mountain meadow. It could have been Kodiack in costume. In the background, snowy peaks framed assorted wildlife and off in a corner, a wagon train found its way through a valley. The jacket of *The Last River* promised "bracing, edge-of-your-seat excitement, heroics of the first magnitude, and passionate romance that add up to a dynamic tribute to the brave souls who conquered the great Northwest." Immediately I knew I would never read it.

Oscar Vargas asked Kodiack a question.

"When you saw Rachel the last time, before you returned to the United States, what did she talk about? What was on her mind? I would just like to know a little about what she was doing before she, she . . ."

Kodiack quickly offered what he could.

"Yes, of course. Let's see. We were in the condo. Rachel, me, and Flores, the all-around butler, valet, et cetera, et cetera. Great man. Does a wonderful job for us. Rachel had been working on her novel, and I had edited a few pages. We talked briefly about the screenplay, but so far there's been no real action on that. I did not understand all the symbolism she was using in her novel, nor did I see its necessity. It is, after all, a genre piece, a whodunit if you will. But she was adamant. Rachel was—is—nothing if not stubborn. She thought she had something to say about a variety of subjects, and that was where we left it. I went to bed, and Rachel and Flores stayed up. Rachel and Flores liked to talk. She practiced her Spanish, and he practiced English. The next morning, she was gone. It was early when I left for the airport. That night I was back in Montana. I didn't know until young Valdez called me that she was even missing. I had no idea."

Old man Vargas hung on his every word, trying to capture a fleeting glimpse of his missing daughter. He nodded when Kodiack finished, and thanked him.

I said, "You know, when I was down there, I didn't see you. Guess you were never on the beach when I was."

"I don't hang out on the beach. I go down there to get away from people, not mingle with the tourists. Not that, uh, not that you were a tourist, Mr. Montez. Rachel did tell me about you. She was quite impressed, actually. Had heard about you from Philip, our neighbor, and she thought that it was exciting to meet a man who actually did business with the court system, cops, and all that. That's what she was trying to write, so you impressed her. Sorry we didn't meet when we were down there. The three of us might have had an interesting conversation, talking about your beautiful city here, Denver, and cops, lawyers, defendants and judges, all that."

"Yeah, maybe. I did meet Flores. You know that?"

"Really? When was that?"

"After you left, apparently. He was quite upset. Claimed that all of you skipped out owing money to everyone in the town. He was not pleased. Looked as though all of you leaving was a surprise to him. What about that?"

The woman from the bookstore reappeared and announced that she really had to close up and get home. Kodiack stood abruptly, gave her a massive hug, and expressed profuse gratitude for setting up the signing. He gathered up his things and we all left through the side door. A car and driver were waiting for him in the parking lot. He gave Oscar Vargas a quick handshake, wished him well, and tried to reassure him again about Rachel's eventual reappearance. He waved at the rest of us. The Vargas men walked in one direction while Rad sauntered off in another, toward my car. I thought Kodiack would climb into his escort's car, but he stopped and walked over to me, smiling. He put his arms around my shoulders and squeezed.

He whispered so that no one else heard him.

"Flores is a conniving Mexican. He was supposed to pay the bills—we gave him the money. If the bills weren't paid, then he made off with our money. I'll deal with him the next time I'm down there. Any more questions, Montez?"

He kept smiling and squeezing.

I wrenched free.

"You answered all my questions. So long."

Later, when I let Rad off at the hotel, I told him that actually I still had a few questions. I just had not wanted to ask them of the pushy writer.

"What questions, Louie?"

"Well, for example, why leave your isolated cabin in the quiet woods of Montana for a tourist trap in Mexico if you want to get away from people? That's one. And, for another, how does Flores go from a 'great man' to a 'conniving Mexican' in the space of a few minutes? What do you think about those questions, Rad?"

"It's like I said, the man is the key to finding Rachel. He's covering up something. Maybe Flores can shed some light on the comings and goings in the condo. Maybe I should go back to Mexico and talk with him again. I didn't spend all the time with him that I should have when I first went down looking for Rachel."

His energy level had stayed high and he fed it with the thought that at last he might be able to do something affirmative about finding Rachel.

"That's a thought, Rad. Flores should have some good stories to tell about Kodiack and Rachel, probably about the whole bunch. He could be very useful."

We sat in silence for a few seconds, digesting what we had picked out of our talk with Kodiack. Finally, I exhaled loudly and clicked my teeth.

"What's with the sighs, Louie?"

"Oh, it's just that I haven't heard such an ugly tone of voice in a long time. It threw me a bit, that's all."

"You mean Kodiack?"

"Yeah. When he decided he had to confide in me. He told me that Flores was a conniving Mexican. I haven't heard the word *Mexican* sound so contemptible since I was a little kid. It was bad, Rad. Ugly bad."

19

◆

The detective's traveling clothes consisted of a light-weight, black, collarless shirt, a pair of khaki pants, and his earring. Very dark sunglasses hid his eyes. The good shoes needed a shine, but they still added a certain touch.

Conrad Valdez caught the earliest flight he could book for Los Cabos. I gave him yet another ride. Flores, the man I had thought might have been a well-tanned North American with Asian eyes, had become the focus of Rad's attention. Rad believed that the servant might dish up more details about Mel Kodiack, and that those details would lead to Rachel. I wished him well, but I was not as hopeful. Sure, I thought, Flores can provide something, but it won't be the answer Rad wants. Too much had happened, and that answer was gone.

The Vargas family checked out of the hotel and traveled to the airport with Rad, crowded into the backseat of my car, insisting on paying for my gas and the parking. I let them. Although they had a later flight, it was obvious that they were tired of the hotel, tired of Denver. They were sullen and quiet on the short trip to Stapleton. Kodiack had offered nothing of substance, and Rad's new Mexican adventure sounded, at best, like another fishing expedition. I anticipated that if the PI did not come up with something more concrete by the time he returned, his expense account would be closed and the Vargases would try to get on with their lives without Rachel.

During the ride, Rad gave all of us the latest bits of information he had picked up. There had never been a ransom demand, nor any word from anyone who might have had contact with Rachel. The performance artist, Isela Vega, had finally surfaced and she had given a statement to the Los Angeles police. Rad had been faxed a copy by his source at the department. Vega insisted that she knew nothing about Rachel's whereabouts, expressed genuine concern, and offered to cooperate in any way she could. The source indicated that Vega was not a suspect.

Rad also had news about Brian Gulf. The screenwriter had been ordered held for observation in a northern California rehab center. He had been picked up in San Francisco, incoherent, beaten, and without identification or money. His future did not look bright.

Nothing Rad said cheered up anybody.

In the cramped backseat, Patricia fidgeted and groaned. Her anxiety level had reached a new high, and I fully expected her to lose whatever she had managed to stuff down her throat for breakfast all over her father and brother.

Jaime Vargas tried to console his father. "Dad, Rachel never wanted you to worry about her. We have to be as strong as her."

I dumped the troubled Vargas mob at the check-in

doors and quickly returned to downtown Denver. Conrad may have been chasing Rachel's ghost, but I had my own to deal with—Charlotte Garcia.

I had to assume that my misgivings about Rad's role in the fire were unwarranted. Although he had lied about the warning and his lack of candor had contributed to the horrible surprise of the fire, I did not hold him responsible. Somebody had tried to shake him off Rachel's trail— the ominous card was proof of that—but that did not mean the fire had resulted from the warning. It wasn't that clear-cut. On the other hand, there was no doubt that Bobby Baca had paid the price of mixing in with the wrong crowd, and it was not much of a stretch to assume that the same wrong crowd had played a part in the torching of the 'Hole. Baca, Charlotte, the fire, Montero. Too many coincidences for me, and, as I had told Baca, I was the guy who didn't trust in coincidence. Certainly Chick Montero had killed Weeds Lopez, probably financed by Albert Kopinski. How could I link Montero to the fire?

Rodney Harrison shook his head.

"No way, Louie. You got to be kidding. The last time I went along with one of your schemes, a guy got shot and the police grilled me for a couple of hours. That was it. You're on your own."

"I can't do it without a partner. You know Montero; I don't. I think I know what went down between Baca and Montero, but I want to try to make him admit it. I'll be the guy in the middle. You smoke him out. That's all. Then leave it up to me. You won't even be involved. Montero won't come if it's just me he hears from. But you, you can get him here because Baca came around asking you for Montero. Montero can see that the thing with Baca is not as finished as he thought, and as tidy as the police have made it out to be, and that you might have something else that puts him and Baca together. He doesn't know. So he'll come around, just to check you out. You don't even have to be there. Just make the call, put out the word. Tell him to meet you at your lawyer's office. Say that Baca had left something with you. He won't know what to think. Then lay low. Close up early and visit that sister you're always bragging about, the one who teaches in Pueblo. I'll take it from there. What do you say, Rodney? For old times' sake."

"Don't give me that old times' sake shit. You ask too much, Louie."

When he finally agreed, I was not sure I was relieved. Rodney Harrison was not the kind of man who would walk away from what I had asked. He had to be coaxed, sure, but as soon as I asked, we both understood he would do it.

Maybe I had gone too far, bitten off too much. My second thoughts had me worried that I should have left the detective work to Rad, and the cops. Maybe Luis Montez, Esq., did not quite have the tools necessary to pull off what I had in mind. Except for the fact that I owed an answer to Bonnie Collins, there was no motivation for me to try to get the truth out of Montero. I did not think that even Charlotte Garcia would have pressed me for a resolution. But she was not around to ease my conscience, and that's where the second thoughts stayed. In my conscience.

I sat in my car, parked in the darkness in front of my house. As I waited for Chick Montero, disconnected musings forced their way into my consciousness. A member of a Denver gangster family, heir to the throne, so to speak, had been executed on his porch several years before—shotgunned as he tried to dig out his keys. The guy had owned a popular Northside bar, a place I had sipped a cool one once or twice myself, and I remembered thinking that it was not right that he should have had his head exploded all over his front steps. Weeds Lopez had died almost on the same spot where my car rested. Not much had been left of *his* head, either.

A car stopped several houses down from mine, in the darkness of a leafy elm that hid the streetlight and arched over the street. A man slowly emerged from the driver's side of the car. I shrank as small as I could in the car, and listened for him to walk past. Stretched across the seat, I peeked through the passenger window and saw his back turn into the path to my house. Montero strolled boldly to the door and knocked. No skulking around the windows, no reconnoitering the perimeter. He did not appear to be wary of any ambush.

I quietly opened the door and climbed out. The door light in the car went on and for an instant I was framed in its yellow glare. Montero turned almost immediately. I walked around the car.

"Chick Montero, I'm Luis Montez. I asked Rodney Harrison to call you."

I stood about ten feet from him. My hand rested on a very small Walther PPK. I had owned the gun for years, but had never fired it at any living creature. I could not even remember the last time I had used it for target practice. I figured that if I had to pull it out of my pocket I was probably dead.

"What's this all about? What you got to do with Bobby Baca? Where's Harrison?"

"He'll be by a bit later. I waited out here because I wanted to make sure you didn't bring any unwelcome pals along. I didn't want to be a sitting duck in my own house."

He laughed. "What makes you think you ain't out

here? Anyway, what do you want? I'm busy, got things to do."

It was hard to make out details in the night, but I could see that he was dressed in slacks and a casual, short-sleeved shirt under a thin windbreaker. He looked to be about my height but with a few more pounds around the upper chest. His neck struck me as incredibly thick.

"Answer a couple of questions and then our business is over. I won't make any trouble for you. I simply need to have a few loose ends tied up."

He laughed again. "What makes you think that you can cause trouble for me? I know who you are. Heard about you. A two-bit lawyer without much of a practice. Not a very good reputation. I don't think you can cause me any trouble at all."

Much as I hated to admit it, he had a point. I played the only card I had.

"I know what happened at the rec center. The night Baca got shot."

"Sounds like you better go to the cops. What's that got to do with me?"

"Like I said, I know what happened. I was there."

There was a brief silence. Around me, the Northside sounds that I had taken for granted in the past were muffled. No one cruised my street, no sirens sounded in the distance. The houses on either side of mine were dark, and quiet.

Montero said, "Get out whatever it is you want to say. I got things to do."

We had slowly worked our way to the porch. Only a few feet separated us.

The words were quick and breathless.

"I think that Weeds Lopez leaned on Baca for money. Weeds was in debt to a very disagreeable man. Weeds had something on Baca and he tried to extort what he could. Either Lopez got killed because of the man he had crossed, or because Baca had decided that he couldn't pay anymore. Baca never had much money, so whatever Weeds was getting out of him must have stretched him to the max. Maybe he thought he had to use whatever cash he did have to invest on insurance that Lopez would really go away."

"So far, you ain't said nothing that I need to hear, or even care about."

I took a deep breath. My lungs filled with the sickening odor from the Globeville dog food factories. My queasy stomach gurgled in the night.

"Let me play this through for you. Kopinski has a very bad temper so Lopez needs to come up with some quick cash. Baca is blackmailed by Lopez because of that song he wrote. Lopez had found out the truth about Baca's most famous bit of writing, the piece that was going to be the center of the new book that he was negotiating. Baca hoped to cash in on the renewed interest in the old movement. He couldn't afford to have anything mess up his deal. He has someone take care of Weeds."

"I don't know anything about what you're talking about. Movement bullshit, negotiating a book. What is all that?"

"Maybe you don't know all the details, but you were in the middle of all this, Montero. You were a link between Kopinski and Lopez, and then Baca. You were one of the players."

"I don't like this, Montez. What a waste of time. I think I'll leave."

He placed his hand inside his windbreaker and made a motion to walk off the porch.

"Wait! I don't care about Baca. Whatever happened to him is not what's driving this, just like it doesn't matter much anymore if it was Kopinski or someone else who bumped off Lopez. I'm not going to go to the cops. Charlotte Garcia was my friend, and I promised another friend that I would get her some closure on Charlotte's death. The fire that killed her. That's all I want to know. Was that something that Baca came up with? Or was it aimed at Baca? That's all."

He stepped back, a few more feet away from me. He did not speak. I tried again.

"You're right about one thing. I can't really cause you any trouble. I don't have proof of anything. I saw a note to Baca. From someone who was blackmailing him about his song. With references to Weeds. But I can't prove that you wrote it. And I won't try. Just tell me about the fire, and Charlotte. What happened?!"

My voice trembled, and I knew that eventually we would be heard by someone on the block. Maybe they would assume it was a married couple's squabble and ignore us. Or they might call the cops, and then for sure I would have to scramble to keep from getting shot by somebody. Images of broken heads in front of my house floated into my thinking.

"Okay, Montez, get this straight. I don't know nothing about Weeds or Kopinski. Those assholes have stayed away from me, and me away from them. And you're way off about this fire. Let's say that something was going on with Baca and Weeds. Fire ain't the way a person deals with those kinds of situations. You got to keep the pressure on if you ever want to get any money out of the mark, and you don't call in a torch for that. But it wasn't exactly a secret that Baca was freaked after that fire. He even went around trying to find me, as if I would get in bed with him! Maybe he thought Weeds had something to do with it, and he took care of Weeds on his own. Who really knows? I don't. That's all I got to say to you, Montez. Don't waste my time anymore."

He moved toward me, then slipped around me as though he had already used too much energy. He was gone into the dark street. I heard a car door open and shut.

I groped for my keys, then limped across the porch. I was unlocking my door when I heard the rustle behind me. I gripped my gun again, and held my breath. Should I rush inside, or bide my time and try to make Montero show himself? Could I outrun a shotgun blast?

"Was it worth it, Louie?"

"Damn! Rodney, you got to quit sneaking up on me like that!"

"Hey, I thought you could use some extra cover. You can't screw around with a guy like Montero. Can't be too careful."

He had been waiting in the darkness too. He had heard the conversation, and had been ready to rush in if I had needed it. It was more than I had expected.

"What are you doing here?"

"Sis couldn't get together tonight. Business with her school for next year, or something like that. She invited me up for the weekend. So since I had extra time, and my place was closed, I thought I'd see what you were up to. Montero gives me the creeps. Did you get what you wanted?"

"I guess. It's starting to make sense."

"If you say so. I don't get it, to tell you the truth."

"Come on in and let's have a drink. Maybe I can explain it."

I had two fingers of whiskey, straight, to calm my nerves, then mixed Rodney and me a couple of Canadians on the rocks.

"The note I found in Baca's things made it obvious that he was getting blackmailed first by Lopez and then by Montero. The way Montero talked tonight, Baca thought, wrongly, that Lopez had tried to get at him by setting fire to the 'Hole. Baca then runs over Lopez."

"But that didn't end it? Montero jumps in where Weeds had left off?"

"That's what I think. Baca was getting squeezed, right at the time when he thought his ship might have come in. Maybe he got tired of it and was going to the cops. Maybe he didn't respect Montero's reputation for anger and carnage. Chick had him killed, I'm sure of at least that much."

"I don't know, Louie. All this just over who actually wrote a song? Must be a hell of a song."

"You got to understand the way Baca thought. In his mind, he was a heroic figure, a man whose past had never been fully recognized, a man who had ambitions to be much more than he had amounted to, but he could never quite pull it off. His song was the one thing that he did that was timeless. 'Pachuco, Low Rider, Xicano.' It summarized the coming of age of a whole generation."

"But that was so long ago. Who the hell cares now?"

"If nobody else, at least Baca did, and so he was vulnerable to guys like Weeds Lopez, and Chick Montero. And if Weeds hadn't been squeezed by Kopinski, this all might never have happened. Plus, Baca was working on a scheme that he didn't want torpedoed by any questions about plagiarism."

"How did Lopez know that Baca hadn't written the song? How did Lopez get involved in the first place?"

"Cool Cal and Donna, the owners of the Keyhole. Cool Cal, and then Donna, had hung out with Lopez over the years. Through them, Lopez must have met Baca. Hell, he was my client because they passed on my business card to him! There have been rumors over the years about the origin of the song, of course. I never paid them too much attention. Took them to be petty jealousy, *envidia.* Another item on the long list of Chicano myths and fables. But I guess Lopez listened closer to the rumors when they were passed around by Cool Cal and Donna. He thought there might be something to it, so he tested Baca, and the poet probably gave himself away. Both Baca and Lopez were at the end of their respective ropes. They took chances and paid the price."

Rodney stood to leave. He finished off his drink.

"You Chicanos. I give up. You fight over songs and what to call yourselves, and yet you got hundreds of kids like Concep Sanchez on the verge of doing hard time. It's a mystery to me, Louie."

I did not respond. My mind was on another question. Finally, when the question had formed as much as it would in my head, I spoke.

"Know what, Rodney? I still don't know where the fire fits in. It could be like everyone's said from the beginning, someone in Globeville looking for a cheap thrill." I said that much, but I kept to myself the rest of the thought: Maybe it did have to do with the card that Rad had found slipped under his door.

"Still more questions? Well, for sure you can count me out on any other plans you may come up with!"

I shook my head. "Don't worry about that. I think I've gone as far as I can. The only other thing I don't understand, is if Bobby Baca did not write 'The Pachuco Song,' then who did?"

"I don't think you'll ever know. The answer to that puzzle died with Baca, and apparently the person who did write it hasn't seen the need to talk about it over the years, so I don't think it's going to happen soon. Good night, Louie. I'll leave you with your questions and puzzles. I just hope Chick Montero doesn't hold a grudge for lying to him about tonight."

I poured one more short drink and got ready for bed. Rodney would not be hassled by Montero. The blackmailer and murderer would not stir up anything that would bring unwanted attention to him. He had tried to squeeze an extra buck out of Baca, and, when Baca had panicked, he had taken care of Baca with a well-placed round of bullets at the rec center. For him, the story was over, and he would move on to other projects. Rodney and I were irrelevant, superfluous to his life. We had nothing more than our assumptions and conclusions, and Montero moved in a world based on solid facts—loan-shark interest rates, the price of having a welsher pay for his debts, and the screams of a dead man shouting his name into the rancid Globeville air.

I went to sleep and did not dream.

My last conscious thought was that I almost had something to tell Bonnie Collins.

20

✦

Jesús Genaro Montez sipped on an iced tea and tapped his foot to the beat of a frantic accordion. The Texas *conjunto* band fronted by Tony Candelaria played all the old favorites, and I could not resist the CD when I saw it displayed in the discount store. From *"Volver, Volver"* to *"Soy de San Luis"* to *"Señorita Cantinera,"* Tony C.'s greatest hits could warm up any party. I had played it for my father during one of his infrequent visits, and he loved it. Of course, Jesús didn't own a CD player, so when I gave up the CD, I had to take him to Kmart and buy him the player. And a couple of other CDs. I called the purchase my Father's Day present, which caused him to roll his eyes, shake his head, and generally act as though I was the tightest son a man could ever have. No pleasing the guy.

"I've done about all I can do for Bonnie, Dad. The stuff with Baca and Lopez explains some of it, but not all. We may never learn the whole truth about the fire, but it will have to do. May Charlotte rest in peace."

"Yes, maybe. Poor Charlotte. A decent person touched by the evil of a few bad people. It makes a man wonder."

I slurped the tea. My father's iced tea never failed to be delicious. If he could just transfer his skill with tea to coffee, he would make me a happy man.

I was about to comment on the tea when he blurted out, "Louie, you should know something that girl, Patricia, told me. I told her I would keep her confidence, but I, I have to tell you. The girl and I, we had talks, you know. When she stayed here, and even when she returned to the hotel, she still came around. To visit. She watched TV mostly, or tried to do some yard work. But every once in a while, she would talk, open up a bit."

Patricia had trusted my father, and I had seen that she tried to lean on him for whatever kind of security he could give her. My father had that way with some people. Patricia had filled in the void surrounding her own father with the wrinkled, kind face of Jesús.

I said, "She must have had a lot on her mind. Her missing sister, her own problems."

Jesús nodded and said, "For one so young, she carries an old person's baggage. There are people who are that way since the time they are children. More serious, with worries ahead of their years. She is one of those. But with good reason, I fear."

I knew exactly what he meant. I added my own conclusion to his observation. "Growing up in that family, it could have gone either way. With so many advantages, she could have done almost anything with her life. And yet, seeing how the old man is, and the brother, I guess the women never had a chance."

He was quiet, thinking over how he would say whatever it was that worked on him. The band kept on with an upbeat, happy rhythm serving as the background for a timeless ditty about crazy love.

Jesús said, "That family—*hacen todo a escondidas.* They trust no one, not even each other. They don't know who they are, that's how I see them. All that money, all that history, and yet they are torn apart by their own private disasters. Patricia told me that she hadn't been able to eat right—to keep food in her body is what she meant—since she had realized the truth about Rachel."

"The truth? The adoption?"

"No, no. Not that. Patricia did not care about that at all. She was speaking about this other thing, this awful thing that she discovered one day when the only ones in the house were Rachel, Jaime, and her. Everyone thought Patricia had left with her father."

He drank some tea. He was uncomfortable and that made me nervous. I had rarely seen Jesús reluctant to say what was on his mind. Patricia had revealed something to him that even he, a man with more than seven decades of experiences in two different countries, in labor camps, mining towns, and big cities, had to work up nerve to spit out.

"She found them, together, and it, it was too much, I guess. She never forgot the scene."

"Together? You mean . . . ?"

"*Sí!* In bed, as though they were not brother and sister. Making love, if such *escándolo* can be called love."

"You're sure, Dad? This is outrageous. Maybe she was saying that for her own mixed-up motives. Maybe—"

"No, Louie. She told the truth. It broke her down to get it out, but that last night she was here, she told me the whole story, and made me promise not to tell anyone. She'd known about it for years. . . ."

"Years! This has been going on for years?"

"I'm afraid so. She found them when she was still a small girl, and Rachel was not that much older. And it continued to go on. It drove Patricia wild, because she knew that it was destroying Rachel. But neither of them could do anything."

"The father? What about Oscar Vargas?"

He shook his head.

"No. Patricia wanted to tell him but Rachel forced her to keep quiet. Rachel loved the old man. She thought such a thing would kill him, or would make him hate her forever. Even though she had no choice. Jaime forced her. She already thought she was less in her father's eyes because of the adoption. She believed that if the truth about her and Jaime came out, it would mean that she would lose what remained of the only family she ever knew. Patricia was torn between her loyalty to Rachel and the terrible things that she knew were going on. You saw what it turned her into."

The music stopped. My father got up from his seat and returned the jug of iced tea to the refrigerator, then told me that he was going to take a nap. I realized I had a few things to finish.

"Dad, I'll be leaving."

"Sí. You can call Conrad from here if you want. Pay me when the bill comes."

When Rad returned my message we talked about his interview with Flores. He reached me at my office just as I was about to review, again, what I knew about Rachel and her disappearance. As I spoke with Rad, I debated with myself about telling him what Jesús had revealed.

Rad dished out the cut-and-dried.

"His story jibes with Kodiack's. Nothing there. I thought for sure that Flores would give me something about the writer. When that didn't pan out, I started over. Showed pictures to Flores. Rachel, Kodiack, Vega, and Gulf. He knew them all except Gulf. Claimed that he had never seen him at the condo."

"That's not what he said when he tried to hit me up for their bills. He specifically included Gulf in the group. And Rad, I got the impression from him that Gulf and Rachel were in the condo on some of the same days."

"Yeah, I know what you mean. He's sure there were two men and two women. Not sure all four were there all at the same time. Said they had some wild times. Parties, booze, drugs. Just that Gulf was not one of them. Yet when I talked to Gulf in person, at first he couldn't remember much about anything, but he also claimed that he never saw Rachel in the condo. But he could be making the whole thing up. His drinking had severely clouded his brain. He didn't remember details, could barely remember what day it was."

"This guy, Flores. Had he worked for Kodiack for long?"

I heard Rad flip through some papers, then the whir of his computer came over the line.

"Let's see. Here it is. Flores, Rudolfo. No. Not that long, a couple of weeks. Why?"

"But this group of people, Kodiack, Gulf, the artist, and Rachel. They had been down there before? This wasn't their first trip to the condo?"

"That's right. Rachel had gone down at least twice before, working on that damn book."

"Those earlier trips would have been before Flores started?"

"Right again."

"But it was always the same group of people—Rachel, Vega, Kodiack, Gulf?"

"Sure. They shared the expenses. They all needed a place to get away, for one reason or another."

"Try this train of thought, Rad. See where it takes you. Gulf is out of it, confused about dates and details. Is it possible that Gulf's memory is so shot that when he told you about a trip to Mexico, a trip when he did not see Rachel, he might have been thinking about one of those earlier excursions? You said he could barely remember what day it was."

"That's it! Gulf must have mixed up an earlier vacation with the time I was talking about, the last trip. I assumed we were all talking about the same week. Everyone agreed that Gulf was down there, so it never occurred to me that his frame of reference and mine were different. That could be right, Louie."

"Maybe you should try to talk with Gulf again."

"I think that's a lost cause. He's locked up, hallucinating. His liver's giving out, dementia seems to have set in, according to what I managed to finagle from a nurse up in the Bay Area. Gulf wouldn't know the truth now unless it poured out of a bottle."

"Then I guess the question for you is, if Brian Gulf was not down there when Rachel disappeared, who the hell was it that called himself Gulf?"

"Flores knows the guy. He spent a couple of days with this second Brian Gulf. I've got to talk to him again."

"Quickly, Rad. Too much time has already passed. We've got to dig this guy up."

"I'll have to cancel my flight. I was supposed to fly back to L.A. in an hour. I'll find Flores tonight, then call you as soon as I finish with him. With me down here, I may have to call on you to do something in the States, get the cops involved, whatever. I won't be able to get back until late tomorrow if I stick around for another go at Flores."

"I think it's worth it. You call if you get something definite."

"I'm on my way. Later."

"Rad! Wait a minute. You have pictures of the Vargas family?"

"Sure. I got them all. The old man, Rachel, Patricia, Francisco, Jaime."

"Show them to Flores. See if he recognizes anybody besides Rachel."

"What for, Louie?"

The moment of truth had arrived but I did not have the nerve. Rad had to be cool-headed, objective. I had already concluded that he was too close to the case. The revelation of Jaime's dirty little secret might send Rad on a wild ride that could end up in a tragedy far greater than what we were dealing with so far. I rolled the dice.

"Just a hunch, Rad. Humor me. Call as soon as you finish with Flores."

He hung up. It was my time to wait. There was no one in Denver except me who cared about what had happened to Rachel Espinoza/Vargas. No one to talk with or compare notes. Just me and my telephone. The Vargases were back in Los Angeles, Rad in Los Cabos, Kodiack on his tour, Gulf strapped to a hospital bed, and Isela Vega somewhere in the netherworld she moved in like a celluloid wisp. And Rachel? The one person who knew for sure where she was had not been revealed. He, or she, could be anywhere, I thought. He, or she, could be in Denver.

I leafed through *The Autobiography of a Brown Buffalo* but I did not read a word. My mind raced over the possibilities. I had a couple of things to tell Rad. I opened the box with Rachel's manuscript and threw in Acosta's book. I would have to tell Rad that I had kept more than one piece of the puzzle from him. When we saw each other again, I would give him Rachel's book and hope that it wasn't too late.

I turned off my desk lamp and sat in darkness. I did not make a drink or search for the long-lost, stale pack of cigarettes. Out of habit, I massaged my knee until I realized that I rubbed without purpose. Somewhere between my late-night session with Chick Montero and my enlightening coversation with Jesús, the pain had subsided to the point that it was no more than an easily ignored dull ache.

The ticking of the wall clock filled the space in my office until I heard it no more and I fell asleep in my chair.

The ringing of the phone jarred me awake. I could not tell what time it was. A thin grayness surrounded me. My thinking soaked in a foggy disorientation from the uncomfortable nap I had taken in the chair. I yanked the phone from its cradle and mumbled.

"Hello. What is it? What?"

My brain had enough juice to expect Rad's voice.

"Luis? Is that you. Is Conrad there? I need to speak to him! Quickly!"

"Patricia? What . . . ? No, Rad's not here. What is it?"

"Oh damn! Where is he? We all thought he would return last night. I have to talk to him."

"He's not here. But I'm expecting to hear from him. What is it? Tell me, godammit!"

"Uh, oh. Tonight. Last night. With my father, and

Jaime. Something happened. I have to let Conrad know. Jaime, he's, he's wild, out of control. I don't understand, but I thought Conrad should know. I tried his house in L.A., but he hasn't returned any of my messages. His office answering machine says he won't be back for several days. I thought that maybe he had returned to Denver instead of coming back here like he had told us. So I tried you. Now, I don't—"

"What the hell is it, Patricia? Tell me. Rad will call me soon. What's wrong?"

"My father collapsed, at the ranch. The strain of everything. Jaime and I were there with him. He had something that he thought we all should know. He said that it was for Rachel that he was telling us. But he was sick, almost babbling. I wanted to take him to the hospital, to call a doctor. But he insisted. Had to tell us. I never knew."

"Easy, Patricia. Just spit it out. We can deal with it, whatever it was. My father already told me what you said, about Rachel and Jaime."

She did not say anything, and I feared that I had lost her. The fact of the outrage had been entrusted to Jesús only.

When her voice returned, it sounded breathless and hoarse.

"Yes. I thought Jesús would tell you. And now. Oh, God. What does it mean for poor Rachel?"

I waited, not pressing anymore. She would tell me; I just had to wait.

"My father told us something that he said he told Rachel right before she disappeared. Before she went to Mexico. He said he had to tell her, he had to get through to her because of her obsession with this Acosta who claimed to be her real father. He said, my father said that many years ago, when he was a young man, he had done what men were supposed to do. That's what he said. Can you believe it? Supposed to do! He had women, affairs, mistresses. Women he met because of his business, or women who worked for him, or his friends. I guess there were many. And one of them was a woman from Mexico, an illegal. A woman my father knew for only a short time. But, but . . . she was Rachel's mother. My father could never admit what had happened, not to anybody, not until tonight. He abandoned her, he ignored her pleas for support. But then after Rachel was born, the woman died. . . . He thought that he had to do something, for the girl, and her dead mother. His conscience worked on him. He adopted Rachel. He adopted his own daughter."

My thought process had slowly found its way back into my head. I blurted out, "Rachel knew about her mother and your father? And then Jaime found out?"

"Yes. He screamed and hollered at my father. I thought he was going to hurt him, hurt all of us. He was nuts! He called my father vile names. Terrible, filthy names. Then he blamed Conrad, saying it was all his fault, blamed him for digging into things that he should have left alone. Jaime said Conrad had put crazy ideas in her head. Said that Conrad should have left well enough alone. I tried to stop him, tried to keep him away from my father. He, he hit me, and my father. My father collapsed. His heart. Jaime stormed out, and I had to get help for my father."

"Your father? What . . . ?"

"He's in the hospital. This happened hours ago. I'm still here at the hospital. Waiting for the doctors to tell me something. I'm not sure he's going to make it. But I thought I should try to reach Conrad, to tell him what's happened. Jaime—has to be stopped. He screamed that he had tried to stop Conrad, that he had done all he could, and it still hadn't worked. He sounded like, as though he could hurt Conrad. I don't know, Louie. I need to talk with Conrad. And you, be careful. Someone has to tell Conrad to watch out for Jaime."

The phone clicked off. The Vargas family did not know Rad was still in Mexico. Jaime had stormed off, vowing to stop Rad from continuing his search for Rachel. From Patricia's words, it sounded as though Jaime Vargas blamed Rad for almost everything that had gone wrong in his life. Patricia thought Rad was in Denver, and so Jaime probably thought the same thing. Jaime could already be in Denver—the flight from Los Angeles took only two hours. He could be looking for Rad. There were only two places Jaime might consider in his search for Rad—my office and the home of my father. I had to reach Jesús.

21

No one answered the repetitive ringing at his house. It was early, the sun only a few inches above the horizon. At six-thirty in the morning, my father should have been in bed or shuffling around in his kitchen making his infamous coffee. He should have answered my call. I dug out my gun, again, and stuffed it into the pocket of an old blazer that I threw over my wrinkled shirt. It was still loaded from my encounter with Montero. I dialed 911 and tried to tell the dispatcher what was going on but I was too mixed up and nervous. Finally, I gave her Dad's address and told her to get some cops over there as soon as possible. Because she didn't seem to see the urgency, I shouted that there had been a shooting.

I planned to race from the Northside to the Westside, joining in the line of rush-hour traffic across the Speer Boulevard Viaduct until I could cut off and take Kalamath into the heart of Jesús' neighborhood.

I jumped into my car and started it up.

Jaime's voice stopped me cold. He said, "Glad you finally woke up, Montez. We've been waiting for a while. Your father here has been complaining about a chill."

They sat in my backseat. A gag fashioned from what seemed to be a towel covered my father's mouth. He wore only a thin, fading robe over a mismatched pair of pajamas, and his scruffy slippers. His arms were free, but he sat on his hands. Jaime Vargas held a gun on him, and must have ordered him to keep his hands under his legs.

Jaime was dressed in the same casual but fashionable style he had sported the last time he had been in Denver. His sweaty face betrayed the noncasual nature of his visit.

"You can't get away with this! Let my father go! Let him out. Deal with me, you son of a bitch!"

He swung the gun at my head and tapped me with the barrel. A sharp crease of pain split the back of my head. Jesús wiggled in the backseat and said something that was muffled by the gag.

Vargas said, "Drive, asshole. Take us to Valdez. He must be in some hotel around here. Find him, quick, or I start in on your old man. Now, Montez!"

I pulled away from the curb and tried to think. I made it to the cross street, then I pointed the car in the direction of the Regency Hotel, straight east on Thirty-eighth Avenue, past the myriad of struggling businesses and homes that I had driven by for years without taking any special notice. I searched for anything that might divert Vargas and give me a chance to get my father out of the car.

People on their way to work crowded into the lanes on the avenue. They maneuvered around buses and slower cars. I found a space in the line of traffic and inched forward, struggling to come up with something. The fire-house came and went.

I tried to get Vargas to talk. Take his mind off my father, whom he watched more carefully than me. He knew he had me at his mercy. I would not do anything to jeopardize Jesús.

"It was so important to you to get Rad off of Rachel's trail that you sent him warnings, took shots at him up in Montana, tried other ways to shut him out. You tried to convince your father to call off Rad by saying that this was just Rachel's latest quirk. You couldn't take the chance that what you had been up to would ever come out, could you?"

"That idiot Valdez! Too much of Rachel! He couldn't take a hint! Not even that damn fire worked. Now shut up and step on it."

Jaime Vargas had claimed another victim—Charlotte Garcia. The words made me sick, but I had to keep him talking to work for time. My heart told me to reach back and grab his throat until it cracked in my hands. My brain made me talk to him.

"That's why you were so concerned about Rachel's manuscript. More worried about it than her. You wanted to find that book. It might have had details about your escapades, your own quirks. Maybe she had put something in it about you and your, uh, appetites."

I did not tell him that Rachel's book had nothing in it that would have hurt him. The enigmatic paragraph that had puzzled me could not have been the basis for evidence of any crime or sin. The truth was that the manuscript represented nothing more than Rachel's dream. It had nothing to do with her nightmare.

He raised his gun and threatened the back of my skull again. My father squirmed frantically, and I wanted him to stop before Vargas gave him the pistol whipping that he so obviously wanted to inflict on me.

The words rolled out of my mouth.

"Acting like Brian Gulf while you were down in Mexico. That was stupid, I think. You could easily have been found out. If Vega or Kodiack had arrived even one day earlier, you would have been revealed for the fraud, the creep you are. Poor Rachel, she must have felt trapped by you. What could she do? You had been using her since she was a child."

"Using her! Is that what you think? Rachel used me, she tormented me, tempted me, even as a girl. That bitch was older than her years. She wanted it, and I gave it to her! Don't give me this crap about my using her! She trapped me, roped me in. Then she wanted it stopped, thought she was going to tell my father, the cops, anyone. Fucking bitch!"

My father had quit sitting on his hands. He moved closer to Jaime.

I said, "That must have been around the time when you concocted this Oscar Acosta masquerade. A good way to keep her under control. Promise her a real father, an escape. Set her up to meet someone in Mexico, then you show up, just for old times' sake."

Jaime Vargas was getting nervous. He had to have noticed that I had slowed to a crawl. Traffic whizzed by us as we stalled in the outside lane. Horns honked and an agitated group of young men behind us flipped us off as they waited for me to move from the intersection. The driver opened his door and stood halfway out of his car.

"Get the fuck out of the way! You idiot! We got to get to work!"

I idled at Thirty-eighth and Tejon. A gas station, an Italian restaurant, the restaurant's parking lot, and a check-cashing outlet sat at the corners. I knew a story about each one of the businesses, including the parking lot. I sensed that we were about to create one more and add it to the lore of the Northside.

Jaime Vargas saw the man behind us. He shouted, "Get moving, Montez! Quit fucking around!"

"You can't think that your scheme to keep Rachel quiet would have worked. She wasn't that gullible."

"It would have worked! She bought it all. On the phone, I could talk her into anything! She even started to think that she talked with Acosta when I hadn't done anything. Phone calls and conversations that I knew never took place. Yes, she was a believer. Until the old man told her the truth about that whore, her mother. She retreated into that book of hers. She lost touch with everything. She, I don't know, she turned into someone else. I was happy when she disappeared."

"What?" I did not understand what he had said.

A banging on the window at my side diverted my attention. The man from behind us had walked to my car. He was hollering and gesticulating. Jaime Vargas twisted his neck to get a better view of the angry man. He leveled his gun at the man.

Jesús whipped his hand out of his robe. He held his old revolver that had gathered dust in his closet for years. He screamed at me.

"Get out!"

Vargas shouted something unintelligible. The two men wrestled on the seat, but there was no way that my father could handle Jaime. I jumped out of the car and slammed the door into the man who had made a point about my driving habits. He fell back. I could feel his friends as they leaped from the car and ran to me. I opened the back door. A loud blast echoed in my already ringing ears. Jaime Vargas rolled out of the back and fell at my feet. Blood flowed from a massive hole in his chest. Jesús held the smoking weapon, powder smudging his shaking fingers.

Everything stopped. The men quit running, the horns quit honking. It was as though a curtain of silence had fallen on the Northside when the bullet had screamed its fatal wail into the morning air.

Finally, a siren screamed from up the avenue. Men, women, and children slowly emerged from their cars to stand around us and stare at the dead man lying on the pavement and the old man sitting in the backseat in pajamas and a robe who would not let go of his gun.

I had a lot of explaining to do. My father would not let me off the hook easily. According to him, I had nearly cost him his life, had made him the focus of intense police questioning, and had made him ruin a good robe. I had to sit and take it all. He was right, in a way, although I thought Jaime Vargas deserved more of the blame. Eventually we were able to talk about what happened in a much calmer fashion. It only took several days.

"You got your gun when you picked your robe out of the closet? And Vargas didn't see you?"

We were in his house. I had a beer in front of me and Jesús sipped on tea. He looked tired and had complained of a pain in his back since the shooting. I had scheduled a checkup for Dad with Dr. Webster, the only doctor he would still agree to visit.

"No. He was too worked up to pay me much attention. I'm just an old guy anyway, harmless. He wanted Conrad. He kept saying that he had to stop Conrad before it was all out in the open. I knew what he meant, but I played dumb. He looked for Conrad all over the house, then got the bright idea that he was at your place, or that you knew where to find him. So he forced me in his car and drove me. Then we waited until you came out. I thought I would be there all day, crouched down on the floor of your car. You sleep so late most of the time."

"Yeah, yeah. You could have gotten killed, Dad. What a wild thing to do."

"Hey, it wasn't my idea! I had no choice. And when I could finally get to the gun—he was going to shoot me, I could see it in his eyes. So I had to shoot first. My ears are still exploding. I can't hear a thing. What a monster!"

"You got that right, Dad. He abused Rachel for years. Tried to cover it up with his impersonation of Acosta. A cruel trick on a troubled mind. When all the truth came out, I think it drove Rachel and him over the edge."

"She started to believe in this Acosta."

"Yes. To the point that she imagined speaking to him at times when Jaime had not played his role as Acosta."

Jesús gave me a questioning look and I knew what he was thinking. Had it been only her imagination?

"Luis, you think she's dead?"

"I don't know, Dad. I was convinced in that car that Jaime had killed her. He had impersonated Gulf in Mexico, and he had deceived Rachel about Acosta. He tried to have Rad called off. He gave Rad warnings, shot at him, used the fire to try to scare him off. Those only made Rad more determined. But now that I've thought about it, Vargas could have done all that because he wanted his sins to stay hidden, under the rocks where they had been with the rest of the filth in his life. Doesn't necessarily mean he killed Rachel."

"And that thing he said in the car. That he was happy when she disappeared. That sounds as though she could still be alive, no?"

"Yes. That's what it sounds like. And yet he could have just been covering himself, trying to mislead us. I noticed something about him whenever he talked about Rachel. The first time I met him, every time, he always talked about Rachel in the past tense. As though he knew she was gone. It bothered me when I heard it. Now I don't know, Dad. I just can't say for sure."

Rad and I eventually talked by long distance. The full, ugly truth had hit him hard, and he could not put all the details together. I think he did not want to see the whole produced by those details.

"So, Rad, Flores identified Jaime as the man he thought was Gulf?"

"Yes. That's when I knew that Vargas had, uh, been the person, who—he was the one."

That was about it. I was ready to wish him well, to tell him to take it easy, and hang up. He needed to say something.

"Louie. I'm sorry I dragged you and your father into this. You almost got killed. If I'd known, I never would have put you in the middle. You—"

"Easy, Rad. It wasn't you. Vargas was a sick man, and a killer. He's paid for Charlotte, and I feel good that I had a part in his payback. You did all you could. Take it easy, Rad. Keep in touch."

He said that maybe he would turn up a copy of her manuscript and try to do something with it—find an editor and work on getting it published. I did not say that I had the last draft she had worked on.

We had avoided talking about Rachel. He would continue looking for her, always believing that he was on the edge of finding her. And, once in a great while, Conrad

"Rad" Valdez and Luis Montez, Esq., might even run into each other again. That thought made me shudder.

I sat at my desk surrounded by the paper that marked my career. Files, legal pads, transcripts. Bonnie Collins had made space for herself in a chair by removing a pile of such paper. She carried her own collection of pages in a slim plastic cover.

"You must be glad that you finally know something about that missing girl. Even though it's not everything."

"She's gone, that's all we know for sure. Jaime is dead and my father is a local hero to all the neighborhood kids. Oscar Vargas is convalescing, the remaining daughter is doing what she can to take care of him, and the truth that had been hidden for many years has been exposed. I hope Patricia Vargas makes it."

"Will that detective keep on looking for Rachel?"

"In his own way, I guess he will. He will always have her at the back of his mind. He'll hear about a woman who looks like her, and he might check it out. A voice in the background will tweak some memory, but when he looks up, he won't be able to put a face with the voice. He will do those kinds of things for years, and never give up hope, I guess. He thinks Rachel is still alive. The only thing I know for sure is that she's vanished, just like her imaginary father, Oscar Acosta."

"You sound like you've missed somebody before, as though you know what it feels like to lose someone."

"Oh, that I know, Bonnie. One thing I've got going for me is experience."

She smiled and opened the plastic cover. Sheets of yellowed pages lay in her lap.

Bonnie said, "When you called you asked about that

213

song. I dug it out of Charlotte's filing cabinet. Years ago she told me she wrote it. The fact that Baca claimed to have written it was never a big deal to her. She gave him the song and told him it was his to do with as he wanted. She wrote it for the movement, she told me, so authorship was secondary, in her political mind-set. She was young and idealistic; we all were back then. I don't think she expected Baca to take credit for it, but when it happened, she wasn't angry. It had been wrongly attributed to him because he gave it to a group of young musicians to sing at a conference. They announced it was his song, and then, after it became so popular and famous, it was too late, really, to correct the record. Not that Baca ever tried."

"And Charlotte was okay with all that?"

"It did cause some friction. But, in one of those things that make life interesting, it also created a bond between them. They would fight and argue, but they always returned to each other for assurance. The song was their link. Baca was very insecure about Charlotte. He feared that one day Charlotte would expose him for the fraud he was, but he needn't have worried. She didn't think that way. He was the one without heart. That's why he ended up with men like Wilson Lopez and Chick Montero."

She handed me the sheets of yellowed pages. Charlotte's handwriting filled the papers. The ink was faded in some parts, and the corners were ragged and torn.

"I want you to have this. It's her original."

She left after we promised to keep in touch, but I think that even as we said it we knew that we would have very little contact in the future. Our lives had moved on, past Charlotte Garcia and Rachel Valdez, and when we met again it would be unplanned, at a public place where a bunch of us gathered for something that had nothing to do with either Charlotte or Rachel.

Charlotte's murderer was dead, and my friend had been avenged. Weeds Lopez's killer was dead, and my client's case was finally closed. Chick Montero, the man who had killed the poet Bobby Baca, walked in the shadows of the Northside underworld. I did not owe Baca anything, I thought. Chick Montero would lean on the wrong person one day, and then his own twisted saga also would be finished. It was a loose end for which I felt no responsibility.

Rachel had vanished into the Mexican night. I remembered her from the beach—lovely, lonely, and waiting for the man who claimed to be her father. She waited for more than just a man. Her search for an identity of her own, roots that she could cling to, had taken her on the same road that had been taken more than twenty years before by the man she thought had returned to claim her as his own—Zeta, the Brown Buffalo, Oscar Acosta. Now they traveled that road together, if not in reality, then as part of the myth that belongs to all those who need something more, who look for something elusive that the rest of us never even miss.

I replaced Charlotte's song in the plastic cover. I opened a locked drawer at the bottom of the desk and placed the song on top of the box that held Rachel's manuscript. My bedraggled copies of *The Autobiography of a Brown Buffalo* and *The Revolt of the Cockroach People* took up a small corner of the drawer. I picked up *Brown Buffalo* and the bent spine opened to the last page.

"And I do not want to live in a world without brown buffalos."

I locked the drawer and dropped the key into an empty coffee cup that had sat undisturbed on a bookshelf for years. I moved the cup to the back of the shelf.

I returned to my paperwork.

215

AUTHOR'S NOTE

◆

I want to thank a few people who helped me with *Blues for the Buffalo*—some without realizing it:

Ilan Stavans, for his excellent research on Oscar Acosta that resulted in his books *Bandido* and *Oscar "Zeta" Acosta: The Uncollected Works,* and for that time he asked me what I thought about the Buffalo;

Reagan Arthur, for her questions and suggestions, always good ones, and the rest of the helpful crew at St. Martin's;

Mercedes Hernández, who has prevented fractured Spanish in all of the Luis Montez books;

Florence Hernández-Ramos, who, because she knows Luis better than I do, can't be thanked enough;

the readers of the Luis Montez stories, who seem to like the guy;

and Rad Valdez wishes to express his gratitude for the invaluable technical assistance of several renowned sleuths including Sonny Baca, Joe Blue, Rafe Buenrostro, Gloria Damasco, Henry Rios, and Cecil Younger.

Finally, *Blues for the Buffalo* is a work of fiction. I made it all up. Similarities between any of the characters and real persons, living or dead, are strictly coincidental. Wise out! *¡No te chifles!*